Praise for Shirley Gould's Books

Shirley not only brings Africa to life but immerses you in a world of both beauty and peril. A gripping story about justice, truth, and the cost of standing up for what you believe.

— SUSAN MAY WARREN, *USA TODAY* BEST-SELLING AUTHOR

Wow, I just finished reading *Sunset Over Swaziland*. I'm crying tears of joy. The ending was like nothing I've ever read or seen in a movie. You are blessed to come up with that. It was so real. God bless you.

— DEANNA JACKSON, DEAR FRIEND, A READER OF CHRISTIAN FICTION

There was one thing wrong with *Sunset Over Swaziland,* it was too short. I didn't want it to end.

— BILLIE JEAN ALFORD, LOVER OF SHIRLEY GOULD'S BOOKS

The Kissing Ball

Shirley Gould

Scrivenings
PRESS
Quench your thirst for story.
www.ScriveningsPress.com

Published by Scrivenings Press LLC
15 Lucky Lane
Morrilton, Arkansas 72110
https://ScriveningsPress.com

Printed in the United States of America

Paperback ISBN 978-1-64917-430-7

eBook ISBN 978-1-64917-431-4

Editors: Karen Tankersly and Denica McCall

Cover design by Linda Fulkerson - www.bookmarketinggraphics.com

All characters are fictional, and any resemblance to real people, either factual or historical, is purely coincidental.

Scripture quotations are taken from The Message, copyright © 1993, 2002, 2018 by Eugene H. Peterson. Used by permission of NavPress.

Chapter One

Everyone wants to be me. If only they knew.

Taking advantage of a lull in her schedule and a much-needed break from the press, Angelica Ward slathered pricey lotion on her skin and let the sun do its thing. She loved the safety and seclusion of her private veranda with a view of a manicured lawn, her late grandmother's flower garden, and a peaceful lake in the distance.

People didn't realize pedestal dwellers could get lonely and have few friends. They didn't understand the constant pressure of living in a goldfish bowl. If they reported about her taking over her grandmother's duties—promoting charities that helped crippled and underprivileged orphans—it might be different. But they wanted to portray her as a spoiled heiress and preferred made-up stories showing her in a less-than-flattering light, which tarnished her reputation.

After squeezing lime into her mother's pitcher of ice water, she poured herself a glass. Using her mother's things helped Angie remember her. She drank half the water and reclined on the cushy lounge chair. Considering tan lines were never apropos for a lady in Dallas' society circles, she wore her strapless, deep-blue, one-piece suit.

Hearing her grandfather, Alexander Ward, conducting a business luncheon on the patio behind the estate, Angie knew he was brokering deals and increasing revenue with every proposal to raise their net worth, which would increase their wealth and draw more unwanted attention. Being the heiress to his millions attracted reporters who circled like vultures.

A pleasant breeze swept the area, sending a loamy smell from the lake bordering their property and clashing with the pungent chlorine from the pool. A pair of cranes took flight into the cerulean sky. Angie slipped on her Louis Vuitton shades and relaxed—until she heard the unmistakable sound of a camera snapping a photo. Jerking into a sitting position, she screamed as the wooden fence cracked and sent a man catapulting through the hedge toward her.

"Paparazzi!"

"Ouch!" He landed with a thud and came up, struggling to protect his camera. Scrambling to get away before security arrived, he reached for Angie's chair to regain his footing.

Angie grabbed the pitcher and swung it at his face. A stream of blood ran from the man's nose and splattered her before the pitcher shattered on the imported paving stones. "Leave me alone!"

The photographer yelped in pain, grabbed his nose, and took off running. James, Ward's chauffeur, chased the man toward the gated entrance of the estate.

When he heard her scream, Tanner Zarello, the maid's son, ran from the pool area, stepping over the broken glass to reach Angie's side. "Angie, are you hurt?"

"No, just shaken. He startled me." She faced Tanner, her trusted friend, and felt safer when he put his arm around her.

Using a linen napkin from the luncheon, he wiped the blood from her face.

"Angelica, are you hurt? What happened?" Alexander Ward reached the scene with Ellis, Angie's security guard, on his heels.

"I'm okay, Grand-Papa." Tears clouded her eyes as she trembled. Her heart beat double time. "Paparazzi again." She held up her hand. "I know what you're going to say—it's the price we pay for having fortune at our fingertips. Maybe I need to move to a foreign country where I'm harder to find. Don't worry, Grand-Papa. Finish your meeting and let Sarah clean up this mess. I'll be fine."

Tanner wrapped another beach towel around Angie and picked up the pitcher. "I think she left an impression on the photographer."

"It's the Ward constitution. She'll come out swinging every time." Ward squeezed her shoulder and kissed the top of her head.

"Ellis, call the police, take pictures of the scene, and document the details. Tanner, get Angie inside so she can clean up." Ward took charge, true to his nature.

James returned, struggling to catch his breath. "He got away. Sorry. He took off through the forest. It looks like he climbed the fence on the other side of the hedge, but it wouldn't hold his weight, so it broke and tossed him onto the veranda."

While Ward spoke with his security team, Tanner put Angie's flip-flops on for her. "Let's get you inside." He slipped his arm around Angie's waist and escorted her to the entrance of her private suite. Holding the door, he waited as she paused to look at the pieces of her mother's pitcher as the water mixed with the splattered blood around it.

"That was Mom's pitcher." Shards of the crystal sparkled, reflecting the sunlight of what would have been a perfect day.

"Sorry, Ang." He guided her inside. "And I hate that he got so close. Being rich and gorgeous makes for great fodder for the gossip rags. Move over, Kardashians. " He used the corner of her towel to wipe some blood off her arm. "You want to sit for a while or head straight to the shower?"

"Let me rest a minute." Still wrapped in her towel, she sat on the leather couch. "Why are you here today? I thought you had appointments in the city."

"Mom had a last-minute shortage of two waiters for the luncheon. I came to her rescue."

"So you need to get back? Go. I'll be okay." She put her hand on his arm. "Finish your responsibilities, and I'll see you later."

He stood. "If you're sure you're okay, I'll check on you before I leave."

"Deal. Thanks, Tanner."

When the door clicked shut, she headed for the shower to wash the lotion off her skin, hoping the warm water would rid her of the fright. She needed to stop trembling.

Tanner walked through the massive commercial kitchen equipped with the best of everything. Their staff could feed a few or a crowd, offering exquisite cuisine served with precision. "Mom, what else needs to be done?"

Maria turned from the sink. Though in her mid-fifties, she was still an attractive woman. "Get a plate and enjoy some of this food. After Ward ends his meeting, we'll begin the final cleanup. Is Angie okay? I saw you run to the rescue when she screamed." She handed him a tall glass of iced tea.

"She was shaken by the paparazzi again. Why don't they give it up?"

"They do it for the almighty dollar. A scoop promises notoriety and big bucks, so they push the limits to get a story." She sat beside Tanner with two pieces of chocolate meringue pie. "Don't leave until I give you a check for today."

"Mom, I came because you were shorthanded. I don't expect to be paid." He cut into his filet mignon. "Good steak, and your au gratin potatoes are the best."

"Thanks, son. All who work the event will be paid, including you."

"Yes, Mother." He winked and finished his lunch. As a single mom, she'd sacrificed so much to raise him. After being hired by Joy Ward, she ran the Ward Estate like a WAC sergeant, making sure every need was met on time and with perfection. Sixteen years of tenure proved she was good at her job.

"I hear voices in the living room. Their meeting must have ended. It's time to get to work. Finish that pie." She took her plate to the sink.

"Slave driver."

She laughed and left the kitchen, barking orders to her team.

With security tightened and paparazzi at bay, Angie ventured into the sunshine, scanned the Ward Estate with her trusty Nikon, and breathed in a mixture of chlorine and flowers. Her grandmother's garden teemed with butterflies. She loved being behind her camera's lens, but her last name often shoved her out front.

"Angie has left the building." Ellis, her security guard, spoke into the intercom at his wrist. "Sound off, guys."

"All clear on the home front," James reported from his post.

"Clear," Andy, Alexander Ward's personal security guard, reported in from the pool area.

"Thank you, thank you very much," Ellis responded in his best Elvis impersonation.

Angie smiled. "Ellis, I'm going to buy you a gaudy white jumpsuit for Christmas." She was glad his love for the king of rock and roll, though humorous, didn't hamper his work.

He gave her a thumbs-up and scanned the property like a watchdog.

"Hummingbirds are hovering around the coneflowers, Ellis." She took the shot and showed Ellis her screen.

"Beautiful, Miss Angie. You're good with that camera."

"Ironic, isn't it? I love photography—the very thing that's making my life miserable. Grand-Pa-pa's money makes me a sought-after subject of every paparazzi's lens. It wouldn't be so bad if they didn't put me in the tabloids with their vicious lies."

"I know, Miss Angie. Your wealth and looks make them think you're older than you are."

"It's surprising they aren't seeking you out, Mr. King of Rock and Roll." She grinned and headed toward Emerald Lake, which bordered their property. Her long black ponytail swung as her flip-flops slapped the sidewalk. When she reached the end of the twenty-five-foot weather-worn dock, a flock of ducks took flight. She raised her camera as they rose toward some cumulus clouds.

The clanging of dishes disrupted the solitude of the setting as the staff cleared the pool area from Grand-Papa's luncheon.

"Hey, Zarello, can you bring that table to this side of the pool?" the caterer called out.

"Sure." Looking buff in his polo shirt and cargo shorts, Tanner lifted the heavy table, unaware of Angie's scrutiny. His Italian blood came through in his looks—black hair, brown eyes, and dark tan skin.

Tanner moved the table, caught her gaze, and waved. Angie took a shot, checked her screen, and returned his wave before he shouldered a tray stacked with dishes.

Lazy swaying grass under a weeping willow caught her eye. After taking another shot, Tanner yelled her name. Right as she jerked around, everything went black.

"Angie!" Tanner dumped the tray and sprinted for the dock. "Ellis, call nine-one-one and get Alexander Ward! Now!"

The paparazzi drone that hit her head was long gone by the time Tanner plunged into the lake to search for Angie. The murky water buried all signs of her. He surfaced, sucked in a breath, and dove again, frantic. Seconds mattered. He plunged deep. No luck. He swam left of the dock and kicked, propelling his body forward until her hair tickled his ankle. He dove deeper and wrapped his right arm around her limp body. Shoving off the muddy bottom of the lake, he swam as fast as he could, pulled Angie out of the lake, and began CPR.

"Ellis, 911?"

"They're on the way."

Water ran out of Angie's mouth when he pressed her lungs. *Yes.* He pressed again, and more water came. Still no pulse. He began mouth-to-mouth resuscitation and repeatedly pressed her heart. No luck. He tried again and again. Seconds dragged by in slow motion.

"Please, God. I need a miracle." His panic soared as sirens

howled in the distance. "Angie, don't give up." He pressed his mouth to hers again and forced air into her lungs.

When Tanner moved again to pump her heart, Angie coughed up lake water, took a deep, strangled breath, and coughed again. Her wide eyes held his gaze as she drew precious air into her lungs. They stared at each other for a long moment as water dripped from his black hair onto her face.

"What happened?" She coughed again.

"A paparazzi drone rammed into your head, and you hit the water."

"And you rescued me?"

"Yep." He felt along her hairline and touched the gash, spilling blood onto the manicured lawn.

"Ouch!"

"You're going to need stitches." He moved her hair and held the gash closed to slow the blood flow.

Siren screams competed with Alexander Ward's voice. "Ellis, take charge. Clear a path for the ambulance. Sarah, pack a bag for Angelica. You know what she'll need. Tanner, what happened?"

Tanner stayed close to Angie, holding her head wound. "Sir, a paparazzi drone hit her in the temple, and she fell into the water unconscious. We could've lost her." Tanner's eyes met Angie's with those last few words.

"She's breathing. You can let her go now." Ward eased out of his golf cart, using his cane for stability on the uneven ground.

"Come closer, sir. There's a serious gash here on her hairline. I'm trying to stop the bleeding."

"Great job, son." He grabbed Tanner's shoulder, giving it a squeeze of approval.

Within minutes, the EMTs moved in and took over, forcing Tanner to let Angie go.

"Can you start here, guys? She's losing a lot of blood." Tanner stepped back. "She was unconscious for about four minutes."

"Hey man, you did good. She's breathing on her own," the tech said as he checked her temperature.

Tanner stood, unmoving, as her blood dripped from his hand. He thanked the Lord she was breathing.

The staff paced the scene, watching and worrying. A tech retrieved a gurney and brought it to the water's edge as the lights on the ambulance reflected on the lake. When a police car joined the scene, Alexander Ward met the officers and filled them in.

Tanner stood sentry until the ambulance doors slammed shut and sirens pierced the air. *Paparazzi.* With his jaw set, he scanned the scene, looking for any sign of the guilty party. A slow burn simmered as he started toward the estate and noticed Angie's camera lying on a coil of rope. He picked it up and stared at the cracked lens. *It was a close call. Too close.*

His drone barely made it back to shore. *That was close. Shoot! I didn't expect her to go to the end of the pier. How could I have messed that up? It would have been a perfect shot for a front-page spread. The boss is gonna be furious.*

He grabbed the drone and hurried to his car. After stowing it in the trunk, he sped away on the rocky back road as sirens screamed in the distance. He maneuvered the forested area, drove through a subdivision, then took the freeway ramp. His cell phone vibrated in his pocket. "Yeah."

"Did you get us a front-page shot? You said she was in the backyard. The lighting and setting are perfect this time of the afternoon."

"I haven't looked at the photos yet. She took a fall, and someone called the paramedics. So I got out of there." A wailing ambulance passed him, heading the other way.

"You moron! That would've been great footage of our princess in distress and you missed it. You blew it again."

"Don't get salty. My drone malfunctioned. Not my fault," he lied. "Let me see what pics I got, Joe, and I'll get back to you." He punched the off button and tossed his cell into the passenger seat. *I don't need him sweatin' me right now. I know the front page is the goal, but Angie is the prize subject. My prize.*

"Can you ask for a pair of scissors and cut the band holding my ponytail, Sarah?"

"Right away." Sarah hurried to the nurse's desk and returned to do as Angie requested.

"That is so much better. Thanks. You're the best." When she rubbed the back of her head, her damp hair fell to her shoulders.

"Angelica, where are you?"

Angie recognized her grandfather's voice before he barged into triage.

"Sarah, bring him in here for me," Angie said from behind the closed curtains where a lab tech stuck her with a needle, trying without success to find a vein. The sterile scene smelled of cleaning supplies and antiseptics. It took her back to her visits to this hospital to see Nana Joy before they said their final goodbyes.

"Sure, Miss Angie." Her trusted assistant hurried to do as requested, her messy bun bouncing as she rushed from the room.

"Grand-Papa, I'm going to be fine. After a couple stitches, I'll be good as new."

He grabbed her hand and patted it, a sign of love. "I'll find out who was behind this." He watched the medical team clean the gash on his granddaughter's temple.

"Doc, how bad is it?" Alexander Ward waited for answers.

"The wound is deep. When we're sure it's sterile, we will suture it closed. A concussion is my biggest concern. I've ordered a CAT scan of her lungs and her head wound. We're starting a strong antibiotic now because of the lake water she ingested."

Angie gritted her teeth as a lab tech made his third attempt to find a vein. "Can I go home soon?" she asked.

"No. Sorry, Miss Ward. You were hit pretty hard. We need to keep you for at least twenty-four hours to watch for fever, headaches, and dizziness. With near-drowning cases, there is a possibility of acute respiratory distress syndrome and lung problems. We want to rule those out. Do you have any questions?"

"No. Thanks, doctor."

The physician wrote something on her chart and turned to the head nurse. "Shave the edge of the gash and flush the area again. I'll be back to suture the wound." He left the area.

Ward's forehead furrowed. "It's best we do as the doctor has advised, Angelica. We can't gamble on your health. You had a close call today."

"But Tanner saved me." She closed her eyes as the technician found a vein.

"Yes, he did." Ward squeezed her hand. "I'll wait outside until they have you in a room."

"Grand-Papa, don't wait around here. Go back to moving mountains. The company needs you. You can bring dinner later. Sarah will stay until you return."

"You sure? I don't mind staying."

"I'm sure. Too many memories haunt these halls."

"Sounds like a plan. My executives for the Waco project are waiting for me at the estate. Sarah, call me if anything changes." He kissed Angie's hand and left.

~

When he returned to the estate, Tanner opened the sedan door for Alexander Ward. "How's Angie, sir?"

"She's alive, thanks to you. They were cleaning her wound and preparing to stitch her up when I left. They're keeping her overnight. The doctor is concerned about her concussion. She'll be fine with some strong antibiotics and bed rest for a few days."

Tanner massaged the back of his neck. "And she's breathing okay?"

"Yes." Ward stared at Tanner. "What's wrong, son? You look pale."

Tanner paused. "Years ago, on vacation in Galveston, Texas, I rescued an eight-year-old boy caught in the undercurrent. I got him to shore and did CPR. I tried so hard, but he didn't make it ... didn't take another breath."

Ward put his hand on Tanner's shoulder. "But today is a different story. Angelica is alive. You can only do your best in each situation. It was too late for the boy, and I'm sorry. He probably panicked and took in too much water. Angelica was unconscious, and you got her out in time. That bad experience put you in rescue mode the second Angelica fell. Glean from it, but don't let it cripple you."

"Thank you, sir. I hadn't thought about it that way."

Ward shut the door of the limo. "I have a meeting to finish. If you need to, we can talk later."

"I'm good, sir. Thanks." Tanner watched him enter the estate. A slight limp slowed his pace. He was grateful that through the years, Alexander Ward had taken meaningful moments with him, spoken truth into his life, and offered him encouragement to reach for greatness.

~

Angie's afternoon was consumed with a CAT scan, breathing treatments, and meds before she was finally assigned a private room.

"The shower felt great, but this bed isn't very soft." She turned, trying to get comfortable.

"It's a beautiful suite and much quieter in here," Sarah said. "You've been through a lot in the last few hours. Try to rest, Miss Angie. A nap might help your headache. I'll be right here."

"Thanks, Sarah." Angie pulled a blanket over herself and relaxed. The meds helped sleep come easy. When she woke, the moon cast its glow into her hospital room. "I feel like I just closed my eyes, but it's already dark outside."

Sarah sat in a recliner with Angie's camera screen close to her face. "Hi, Miss Angie. How do you feel?"

"Like I drowned, and life was forced into me." She pushed herself further up in the bed. "Is that my camera?"

"Yeah, Tanner brought it while you slept. He gave me the camera, put daisies on your food tray, then just watched you breathe." Sarah turned the camera off.

"He didn't say anything?"

"No. He just stood there a while, then slipped out of the room."

"I thought I lost my camera in the lake." She pushed a button to raise the head of her bed.

"You're an amazing photographer. I hope it's okay for me to look at your photos. I was hoping you got a shot of the drone that hit you, but you didn't." She handed Angie her Nikon.

Angie checked the camera for damage. "I'll need a new lens, but the body looks fine." She held it toward Sarah. "Tanner saved me today."

"I know, and we're thankful." Sarah retrieved the camera case, put Angie's Nikon away, then handed her a glass of water.

"You said we're thankful. We who?"

Sarah walked back to the recliner, wearing a sheepish expression. "The staff. We talk about you and Tanner, and we're rooting for you two to get together someday."

"Really? I didn't know." Angie smiled. *That would be fine with me.* Being in Tanner's arms twice in one day had turned her growing infatuation into something deeper—much deeper. His touch created an urgency, a strong desire to win his heart. The look of panic in his eyes spoke volumes, and his caress held unspoken messages. She didn't want him to let her go. Ever.

That look was a game-changer, bringing her buried feelings for him to the surface, making her wheels turn. Her new goal—happily ever after with Tanner—could be reachable. If she started college courses early, tested out of as many subjects as possible, and took heavy course loads, she could finish her BA degree and a Master's in record time. She could pursue her career, live up to her grandfather's expectations, and catch the man of her dreams in the process. But for now, she'd keep things as they were and not risk the friendship they shared.

"Anybody hungry?" Alexander Ward's smile brightened the room. His tie had been removed, but his designer suit spoke volumes about his status. Though the gray at his temples denoted wisdom, the laugh lines at the corners of his eyes reflected the happy years he'd enjoyed. His looks turned heads, but he only had eyes for Nana Joy, who'd passed six months before after a brave battle with cancer.

"Maggiano's takeout. They doubled the order. Sarah, take some with you," Angie insisted. "Thanks, Grand-Papa. I'm hungry."

Sarah pulled Angie's rolling table closer and began preparing her dinner. "Mr. Ward, which one is yours?"

"The lasagna." He removed his suit coat.

Sarah arranged his meal on a table in the suite and opened Angie's food. After getting them set, she left for the evening, taking home a serving of some shrimp Alfredo.

"How are you feeling, Angelica?" Her grandfather stood by her bed, his brow furrowed.

"I have a headache, and the gash throbs, but the doctor said I'll be released tomorrow with antibiotics and orders for three days of bed rest."

"I've been thanking the Lord. You're all I have left."

"And I'm not going anywhere, Grand-Papa. You're stuck with me. Now let's eat."

"Good idea." He made himself comfortable in one of the recliners. "Are you past the shock of what happened this morning?"

Angie stirred her Alfredo, letting the steam rise from the dish. "The photographer invading my space on my veranda made me mad. But my trip into the lake shook me to the core. It wasn't like my life flashed before me, but it did bring some things into perspective."

"Into perspective? I don't understand." He cut his lasagna into pieces.

"As they worked on me, I did a lot of thinking. I want to make a difference with my life. If it's okay with you, I'd like to rush my education." She took a bite as he digested her idea.

"What do you mean by 'rush your education'?"

"With a November birthday, I started school late. Then, I lost over a year of my life when Mom and Dad died, and I endured those surgeries. I want to make up for lost time."

"Does it bother you to be two years older than your classmates?" He watched her face.

"Sometimes. Especially now. If things had happened differently, I'd be further along on my education track." She noticed his look of concern. "It's not your fault. However, I only lack a few credits to finish high school. If I apply myself, I'll still walk with my class in the spring. I'd start taking college courses right away. With my grade point average, I can test out of some courses, putting me farther down my degree path."

He paused and wiped his mouth. She watched him take a drink of tea. "What do you think?" she said.

"Would you be overloading yourself? It could be an extreme workload."

"Southwestern University has an online track of courses I'd utilize. If I see it's too much for me, there's an opportunity to withdraw from classes." She popped a shrimp into her mouth and savored the morsel, giving him time to think. "Do you care if I try it?"

"I see no problem as long as you pace yourself."

"Thanks, Grand-Papa." She twirled her noodles, enjoying the smell of Alfredo sauce as she loaded her fork. "I have another request."

He smiled. "Has your mind been working double time since your dip in the lake?"

"Well, maybe. I've also been thinking about Christmas."

"Christmas? It's a bit early, don't you think?" He reached for his tea.

"Yes, but we need to plan. Do you mind if I change a few things this year? I want to put up a children's tree for your office staff party. We could have their names on ornaments filled with gift cards for the kids."

"I think some change is beneficial." He took a bite of garlic bread. "It sounds like a great idea. I'm good with it."

"My second request is a bit of a stretch." She caught his gaze. "Would you be willing to ask Vice President Saitoti from Kenya to send us a kissing ball from the Mt. Kenya area? If he could have it here by December first, we could incorporate it into our decorations."

"I'm afraid I'm at a loss. What's a kissing ball?" He closed his food container and placed it in the sack.

"When we were at Mountain Lodge at the base of Mt. Kenya, our driver, Peter, showed me a round green growth in the trees. He called it the 'kissing ball.' When I asked why he called it that, he said in America it is called the 'miss-toe plant.' It took me a minute to realize he meant mistletoe. He said it held Christmas magic. The vice president has greenhouses and exports thousands of roses to Europe each week. He would send it to us if you asked him. Will you do it for me?"

"I've had conversations with him recently about some business matters. I don't think he would mind. I'll ask him if it would make you happy, Angelica."

She pushed her rolling table away. "It does. We need a few changes to help us through our first Christmas without Nana Joy."

He stood and put her empty plate in a sack to discard on his way out. Gathering his things, he stepped to her bedside. "You need to rest. Ellis is here, So relax and get some sleep. I'll see you tomorrow."

"Good night, Grand-Papa."

He kissed her cheek and left.

Angie turned toward the window to watch the stars poking holes in the darkness. He was going to order the kissing ball.

She smiled. Kissing Tanner would be amazing. Christmas couldn't get here soon enough.

~

Tanner slung his duffle into his Hummer SUV and shut the door harder than he intended.

"Did you go to the hospital?" Tanner's mother handed him some snacks for the road.

He opened the container and shoved a chocolate chip cookie into his mouth. "Yeah, she was asleep. I just needed to make sure she was okay."

"Do you have feelings for Angie?" Maria paused. "She lives in a bubble. Bodyguards have been her constant companions since the car wreck that ended her parents' lives, and I'm not sure she's had any relationships."

He eyed her for a few seconds. "Are you worried about me, or her? She's my friend, and I'm aware of the bubble she lives in. Look where we're standing, Mom. I know which end of this estate I come from. With a proper education and some professional success, I hope to be worthy of her affection." He paused and let out a deep breath. *Someday.*

"Angie has been through a lot," he continued, "and I've walked through most of it with her. I won't risk destroying the camaraderie we share by letting feelings grow between us. Don't worry, and tell your crew of matchmakers to take it easy." He hugged her goodbye.

She kissed his cheek. "I'll tell them, but it won't do any good. Drive carefully. It looks like some thunderstorms are headed our way."

He tossed his computer bag into the back seat, slipped behind the wheel, and cranked his truck. With a wave, he left the estate. As his older model Hummer ate up the miles, his mind replayed the afternoon. *The paparazzi have to be stopped. They got too close today.*

He'd talk to her bodyguards about keeping her safe. Extra measures needed to be implemented. He'd frequent the estate and be a loyal friend. He'd never desert her like his dad had done to him and his mom years ago. That pain had never subsided. It never would.

Chapter Two

Getting cozy in her bed felt divine. Angie enjoyed the perks of her puffy ice-blue comforter and satin sheets as she reclined in her adjustable canopy bed. She breathed in the fragrance of a cinnamon candle and reached for her TV remote when her cell dinged.

"Hi, Angie. How many stitches did it take? Or did they use duct tape to put you back together?" Tanner sounded like he was walking.

Angie laughed. "Ha ha, you're so funny. I have a splitting headache, and my wound throbs with each heartbeat. I have several dissolving stitches inside and seven on the outside. I'm glad my hair will cover it."

"One second you were there—then you were gone. Don't do that again. You scared me!"

"I'm sorry. I didn't mean to. Thanks again for jumping in."

"Sure. Anytime. I've got a class. Stay out of trouble. We'll talk later."

When he ended the call, Angie laid her phone aside and pulled a daisy out of her arrangement, twirling it in her fingers like Meg Ryan did in *You've Got Mail*. Just as Meg had contemplated changes in Tom Hanks in the movie, Angie's thoughts focused on Tanner—her tall, tan, tough but tenderhearted, tried and true best friend. Sure he came from the workers' quarters at the other end of the estate, but she didn't care. Staring into his handsome face while he hovered above her body as lake water dripped from his hair, it seemed he didn't want to let her go. *Is this just wishful thinking? Am I reading too much into the moment? Maybe it was his response to having to save me.* She twirled the daisy as she considered the possibilities.

For years, she'd dreamed of a romantic ending with Tanner. He'd been Prince Charming to her Barbie, her partner when she took dance lessons and her cohort in crime during their teen years. But this near-death experience brought her future into focus. *Happily-ever-after with Tanner Zarello—that's my heart's desire.*

With time on her hands, she spoke into her remote, *"You've Got Mail."* The movie fit her mood and would keep her still for the duration. A cold Coke and some cookies helped. As the credits on the screen rolled, she reached for her laptop and brought up the website for Southwestern University. It was time to put her plan in motion.

As she perused the course descriptions, her cell dinged. She put it to her ear.

"Hey Ang, about fall break. You want to take the jet skis out once more before they're stored for winter?" Getting straight to the point was Tanner's way.

"Sure, that's a good idea."

"My roommate may come with. You can show off your billiard skills."

"You want to bet on the game?" She smiled, knowing she could beat him any day.

"Nope. You cost me too much money."

Her laughter increased when he ended the call.

Angie had kept her answers short, not wanting to sound too eager, but she pulled up the calendar on her phone and started counting the days. Time with Tanner escalated her heart rate. She'd have a list of activities to keep them busy—to keep Tanner close.

"Miss Angie, your lunch is ready. You want it here on your bed tray, or do you want to sit at the table?" Sarah brought a bouquet of mixed flowers into her room and placed them on her dresser.

"I'll come to the table. Who sent the flowers?" Angie put her hair in a messy bun, being careful with the stitched area, as she slipped out of bed.

Sarah handed her the card on the pick.

"Hmm, Mason Malone from Ward Enterprises. Grand-Papa must have said something about my swim in the lake." She slipped her feet into her slippers.

"He probably did. He was pretty upset. Mason is good-looking, and I'm sure he's loaded, but he doesn't hold a candle to Tanner. Your lunch smells good. Your grandfather wants to have dinner with you. I hope that's okay, because I already confirmed your 'yes.' I'm heading back to the office. See you later." Sarah hid a smile.

"Sarah, you're not fooling me. I noticed how you slid that Tanner comment into your diatribe." Angie eased into a chair at her glass-topped dinette table.

Sarah attempted to hide her smile. "Enjoy your lunch— then back to bed for you, Miss Ward. The doctor wants you to rest. Your meds are by your plate."

"A nap does sound good. My head's throbbing. Be sure to check my email, Sarah."

"You got it." Sarah pivoted, her ponytail bouncing as she headed in the other direction.

Promptly at six o'clock, dinner was served in the dining room of Angie's suite. The formal setting of white wainscoting with burgundy walls created a rich atmosphere—perfect for Alexander Ward, who entered right on cue.

"You feeling better?" He made his way toward Angie.

"Yes, my headache has subsided a little."

After kissing her on each cheek, he pulled her chair out before taking his seat.

"You're limp is more pronounced tonight, Grand-Papa. You okay?"

"It's arthritis, Angelica. It acts up when the weather is changing. A cold front must be moving in to cool us down for July fourth weekend." He dismissed the subject as he shook out the folds of his cloth napkin.

Angie shook her head. "You're impossible. You take care of everything and everyone but yourself." She laid her linen napkin across her lap. Having changed into the proper attire for dinner, she enjoyed her grandfather's smile of approval. "What's for dinner?"

"I don't know, but it smells spicy."

Edward, Ward's butler, placed tortilla chips, queso, guacamole, and salsa on the table. "Mexican fare. I hope it meets your approval."

"Thank you, Edward. It looks great." Ward reached for Angie's hand and prayed. When he said "amen," Angie grabbed a chip and dipped it into the guacamole.

"Edward, tell Maria this is really good." Angie reached for another chip. "So, Grand-Papa, what's up?"

"What do you mean, my dear?" He tried the queso.

She finished her bite. "You usually have something to discuss when you have dinner with me at my end of the estate."

"Can't I just want to spend time with you?" He smiled.

"Sure, but we do that at your end of the mansion." She leaned back for Edward to serve their entrée. "Chicken enchiladas. Yum. Can you smell that perfect mix of spices?"

"I do." He paused as Edward placed his entrée in front of him. "Well, you're correct. I do want to talk to you. While I was discussing business with the vice president of Kenya, I ordered the kissing ball for you."

"Thank you. It's going to add the perfect touch to my Christmas decorations."

"You're welcome. I actually need to go to Kenya. Will you go with me? I'm purchasing a piece of land and must obtain a mining permit." He picked up his knife to cut his food.

She sipped her water and returned the goblet to its coaster. "I'd love to go. What are you mining this time?"

"Tanzanite. It's rare and quite valuable. They usually find it only in Tanzania—but a pocket of the gems has been located in Kenya along the coast, south of Mombasa."

"So you're going to snatch it up before someone else does. I don't blame you. I love it there. When do we leave?" She lifted her fork and blew on a steaming bite before putting it in her mouth.

"I had my assistant check your school schedule, and we'll be traveling during your fall break." He took a bite of enchilada.

Angie started choking when panic stole her breath. She swallowed, then coughed a couple of times. Reaching for her water, she gulped a drink.

"You okay?" Ward leaned forward, took her water goblet from her shaky hand, and put it back on her coaster.

"It just went down the wrong way." She took another sip of water and cleared her throat. *This is not good. I'm spending fall break with Tanner.* "I'm okay now." But her head wound was throbbing again. *I need to go back to bed.*

"Your passport is up-to-date." He finished his enchiladas. "I checked it."

Since she had traveled with him on other fact-finding missions, he automatically assumed she was on board with the trip. She loved Kenya, but missing fall break with Tanner wasn't ideal.

"I appreciate this, Angelica. You need to be acquainted with the vice president and his staff. Someday, I want you to lead our overseas acquisitions."

"Sure, Grand-Papa. I would love that assignment." She pasted on a smile.

During their dessert, he talked about her future possibilities in Ward Enterprises. The flan Edward served disappeared without her tasting it. Once her grand-papa bid her goodnight, she readied herself for bed in slow motion, keeping the lights dim to help with her mounting headache. Having to fake excitement about the trip pulled at her like a taffy being stretched. What was she going to tell Tanner? Would he care if she went? Since the EMTs had taken over, Tanner had kept his distance. Was she imagining his interest?

Tanner stretched out on his twin bed in his loft apartment and called Angie.

"Hi, Angie. What ya doing?"

"Just schoolwork. I've got stacks of books this semester."

"Yeah, me too. I'm anxious for fall break. Campfire and s'mores must be on the agenda."

"Well—about that. Grand-Papa planned a trip to Kenya during fall break and asked me to go. I'm sorry, but I won't be here. I'll miss the s'mores, our jet ski race, and beating you at billiards. Sorry, Tanner."

"Bummer. Well, it's okay. I have plenty of work I can do. I've got some reports due before Christmas break."

"So you'll work?" She paused. "I'll miss our fun times."

"Yeah, me too. We'll talk before you leave. Have a good trip."

"I'll try."

Tanner punched the off button on his cell and gazed out the window, watching raindrops trail down the pane.

"Hey, man. You look like you've lost your best friend. Don't worry, I'm still here." Dylan Calloway, Tanner's roommate and best friend, dropped his backpack on his bed. "What's up?"

Pocketing his cell, he turned. "Angie's going to Kenya and won't be there for fall break."

"You care about her, don't you? I can see it." He took a soda out of their mini-fridge and popped the top. Their loft-style apartment was small but adequate for their college lifestyle. And it kept expenses down.

"Yeah, we're close friends." Tanner took his laptop out of his book bag and powered it up. He tossed his pillow against the headboard and found a comfortable position on his bed.

Dylan took a long drink of his Coke. "You going to finish your thesis during break?"

"That's my new plan."

"I think I'll visit my family, then. Can I go with you another time?"

"Sure, but you've got to see this place. And I wanted you to get to know Angie."

"Aren't you taking a chance?" Dylan crushed his Coke can and tossed it into the trash.

"A chance? What do you mean?"

Dylan grinned. "One look at me, and you'll be history."

"I told you we're just friends." Tanner threw a pillow at Dylan, hitting his target.

"And I don't believe you." Dylan laughed.

Using a pushpin, Marco put another eight-by-ten glossy of Angie on the wall of his two-bedroom house in a seedy, run-down suburb of Dallas. He stepped back and smiled. *Perfect.* He kissed his fingers and put them on her lips in the photo. His cell vibrated in his pocket.

"Hello," he answered, keeping his eyes on the latest trophy he'd added to his collection.

"Got a tip for you. Ward and his granddaughter are flying out this afternoon. British Air, flight BA 194, leaving around four." Joe hacked into the phone. "So get there and use the crowd as camouflage to take your shots. Let's put something in Sunday's paper. International travel peaks interest from our readers."

"You got it, Joe. I can slay it. Expect the pics tonight." Ending the call, he grabbed his keys, slammed the door behind him, and headed to the airport. *Where are you going, pretty girl? Better yet, when are you coming back?*

Traffic was relatively light from the Ward Estate to DFW International Airport. Angie relaxed in the limo and watched the landscape rush past their window. "October is in the air. Look at the leaves, Grand-Papa. They've changed color in the last few days," Angie said.

"The last cold spell painted the landscape earlier this year." He checked the flight number on his itinerary. "James, we're flying British Air."

"Yes, sir," James spoke as he changed lanes to take them to the right departure gate.

After arriving in their limo, a photographer snapped their photo several times as they were ushered to the first-class line. With special treatment, their wait was expedited. Angie and Alexander Ward relaxed in the British Air club in short order. Alexander sent a couple emails to his assistant while Angie perused the available refreshments.

"Grand-Papa, I got you some snacks. Would you like some tea?"

"Yes, please." His eyes didn't leave his phone.

After serving him, she sat in one of the comfy chairs and propped her feet on an ottoman. "You okay?" Angie tasted her cheese and crackers as she watched him.

"I'm good." He patted her hand.

She looked at his profile. "Your laugh lines haven't shown in a while."

"Sorry, my dear. Losing your grandmother has taken a toll."

"I understand. She left a void nothing could fill. Grand-Papa, we don't talk about this much, but in my psychology class, we're studying the five stages of grief. I think you're stuck." Angie stirred her ice water, allowing the lime to flavor her drink.

"Stuck? You're going to have to explain." He pocketed his phone.

"Sure. But first, I'll ask again. How are you doing?"

"I have tough moments, lonely times. Sometimes, I think I hear her voice. Then I have to face the fact that she's gone. It's then I get alone and weep. Pretty sad, huh?"

"It's normal, Grand-Papa. They say it's like having congestive heart failure, where the fluid builds up around the heart, and it has to be drained. Crying helps. It makes you feel better. Grief builds up in the same way, and you have to cry it out. Then you feel better for a while. Sometimes you feel guilty for feeling better, but then you start the process over again."

"What you're saying makes sense. That's where I am." His smile didn't reach his eyes.

Angie laid her head on his shoulder. "Well, you're not alone. I'm here."

"That does give me comfort, my dear."

Angie watched people come and go as flights were called. She tried to be excited about the Kenya trip, but her heart still longed to spend time with Tanner.

Ward checked his watch. "It's time, Angelica. They should allow us to board when we get to the gate."

"Africa, here we come." Angie grabbed her carry-on and patiently followed her grandfather, who walked slowly with his trusty cane.

After enjoying first-class comforts as they flew over the ocean, Angie put her leg rest down and gathered her things. "We're making our approach. I hope this is a profitable venture, Grand-Papa. Ten thousand miles is a long way from home."

"Don't stop trusting me now. Have I ever led you astray?" Ward smiled and put his seat in the upright position.

Ending their two long flights, the plane made a bumpy landing in Nairobi. After passing through customs and retrieving their luggage, one of Vice President Saitoti's men approached, took care of their luggage, and ushered them forward.

"Welcome to Kenya, Bwana Ward. I trust your journey was pleasant."

"It was long but comfortable. Thank you for asking." Alexander Ward stuffed his passport into his suitcoat pocket.

"I've taken the liberty of having your hired van waiting at the door. It is parked by the curb just ahead. The vice president is expecting you in his office at ten o'clock tomorrow. Does that fit your itinerary, Bwana Ward?" He opened the door of their van.

"Yes, we can make that appointment time. Thank you for such a warm welcome to your fine country."

"My pleasure, sir." He closed the door, assisted with loading their luggage, and stepped back, statuesque, until they pulled away.

"Bwana, my name is Martin," the driver said. "Your destination is not far. I will get you there with much haste."

"Thank you. Our journey has been long."

Angie pulled her blouse away from her skin. "It's hot and humid in Nairobi, Bwana," she said to Martin.

"Yes, Dada, it is rainy season in Kenya. I trust you brought an umbrella."

"I did, but I hope I won't have to use it."

Within fifteen minutes, their luggage was unloaded at a five-star hotel, and their rooms were assigned.

"A great hotel choice, Grand-Papa. I love African art blended into modern comfort. Who would expect plush carpets in Kenya?" Angie moved toward her room next to his. "I hope you rest well."

"You too. See you in the morning."

Ole Serena Hotel, a five-star establishment, was constructed on the edge of the Nairobi game park, ten kilometers from the international airport. Cape buffalo grazed near the outdoor restaurant, where Angie enjoyed an amazing breakfast buffet next to a birdbath extending the length of the restaurant. An awning of clay tiles kept the morning sun at bay.

"Grand-Papa, there are giraffes in the distance."

Ward sipped his coffee. "You love it here, don't you?"

"Yes, I do. Nana Joy said there was a certain magic about this country. I agree." She took another bite. "So, what are we doing first?"

"We're purchasing a piece of land with a tanzanite mine on it. The process has been shortened since we bought the property in Kenya when we acquired Paradise Inn, our resort on the coast." He motioned for the waiter to refresh his coffee.

"Don't we need the deed before you request a mining permit?"

"That's correct, but Vice President Saitoti is helping expedite the process for us because the mine will eventually fill with water. We're in a race against time." He sipped his brew.

"Then we better get this show on the road." Angie pushed away from the table.

He held his hand up to stop her. "I need to make a call to the States. I'm calling in some reinforcements. Another set of eyes on this project might be a good idea. Have some fruit and finish your tea. Meet me in the lobby and request our luggage to be loaded."

"Sounds great. I'll get more of their juicy pineapple and meet you there."

"Dole grows their pineapples in Kenya in an area called Thika not far from Nairobi." He signed the bill to their room. "Some of the Tarzan movies were filmed around a waterfall in Thika."

"How do you know so much about this country?" She stood.

"Just trivia acquired on my frequent trips." He finished his java and left to make his phone call.

Angie watched some impala grazing in the game park as she finished breakfast and drank a steaming cup of Kenyan chai. As a pair of lovebirds played in the birdbath, her mind returned to her handsome best friend. Tanner would love this place. *Maybe ... someday.*

Dressed in a jacketed sundress, Angie put her hand in the crook of her grandfather's arm, covered with a suit coat. Dressing for success was appropriate worldwide. Their footsteps echoed down the long hallway of painted concrete floors and shiplap walls. Despite an early morning rain shower, a dusty smell hung stagnant in the air. They stopped at a carved wooden door. A uniformed guard checked their visitor passes and then knocked on the door, opening it when summoned.

The vice president's office appeared stoic, with its tall ceilings, low-hanging fan, mahogany desk, and straight chairs. Tea had been prepared for them in a traditional Kenyan tea set displayed on a wooden coffee table.

Alexander stepped aside and allowed his granddaughter to enter.

The vice president ended a phone call, stood, and circled his desk. "*Karibou, Rafiki yangu.* Welcome, my friend. I'm so glad to see you."

Vice President Saitoti embraced Alexander Ward.

"It has been a while," Ward said. "I'm glad to see you are in good health. You remember my granddaughter Angelica? She was quite young on her last trip to your country." He turned, allowing Angie to greet the vice president.

"Please be seated and enjoy some tea." Saitoti sat across from Ward as his aide prepared the brew on the small table between them. "Help yourself, and tell me how you have been.

I know your heart is heavy with the loss of Mama Joy." He blew his tea before taking a sip. "You have been in my prayers."

Angie added sugar to her cup and stirred without clanging her spoon on the ceramic mug. The mixture of warm milk, lots of sugar, and a little tea reminded her of the chocolate-flavored milk she enjoyed as a child. "Mama Joy loved Kenya. Her trips to your country gave her many wonderful memories. Our hearts are saddened. She's greatly missed," Angie said.

"Joy traveled to Kenya with me in the past, but I'm happy to have Angelica on this trip. I've asked her to listen and learn the details of these transactions so she can do business for Ward Enterprises in the future. She's being groomed to take an executive role in my company."

"Following in your footsteps, she will change the world." Saitoti reached for a folder on his desk. "I'm glad to assist you in this land matter. I have the forms you need. I've informed the Mombasa office of your visit and asked them to have the survey ready when you arrive and not delay your progress. The land purchase needs to be completed while you are in Mombasa, and the mining permit can be filed here in Nairobi upon your return." Saitoti handed the file to Ward.

"Your work has expedited this process. It has saved us weeks of labor." Ward perused the forms before handing them to Angie. He leaned forward, placing his elbows on his knees. "We are bringing people from the States to lead the project, but we'll be hiring Kenyans as miners and guards. We want to help your economy by offering jobs."

Saitoti finished his tea and placed his cup on the wooden table. "We appreciate this good news, but I would expect nothing less. You have employed Kenyans at your resort on the coast for years. Please let me know if you need more assistance with these land matters."

Alexander Ward sat forward, rubbing his aching knee.

"Thank you for seeing us today." When Saitoti stood, he and Angie did the same, signaling the end of their meeting.

"I have a special request before you leave," the vice president said. "I'm hosting a reception next Sunday evening at the Nairobi Hilton for my daughter. She has just accepted a marriage proposal to a fine young doctor she met in the States. I would be honored if you could attend."

Ward looked at Angie, and she nodded in affirmation.

"We have a late flight to the States, but it would be our joy to attend the reception before we go to the airport," Ward said.

"It's a semi-formal dinner at seven in the ballroom at the Nairobi Hilton Hotel. *Asante, Rafiki yangu.* Thank you, my friend." He put his hand in Alexander Ward's open palm, a sign of friendship in Kenyan culture. "I will anticipate our time together."

Ward released his hand and slapped his back in an American old-boy fashion. "It will be a good time."

Angie shook hands with the vice president. "Thank you for your time. I know your schedule is full."

Saitoti's cell phone rang. He retrieved it from his suit coat pocket.

"See you next Sunday," Ward said as he closed the vice president's door, giving him privacy for his phone conversation. He led Angie down the long hall and out of the presidential building to their waiting van. "Take us to Wilson Airport, please," he instructed Martin, their driver.

"To Mombasa now?" Angie said.

"Yes, to Paradise Inn." Ward made some notes as they drove through Nairobi.

Since the air conditioner couldn't keep up with the exhaust fumes, motion sickness threatened Angie. She downed a Dramamine and watched the road to ease her stomach. Sights of dirty children begging from passengers stalled in the traffic tugged at her heart.

"They're starving, Grand-Papa. Look how many there are. So sad. What a contrast—beautiful high-rise buildings surrounded by hungry beggars."

"It's the plight of third-world countries, my dear."

Angie hung on as they hit one pothole after another, passing scrawny dogs chasing dirty orphans. Driving on the opposite side of the road with the steering wheel on the wrong side of the vehicle added angst to the traffic experience.

Old buses, brightly painted vans, and way too many cars filled the streets. Vendors moved from car to car selling their wares—everything from sunglasses, bananas, photos of the president, which were required in every business, and bright-colored steering wheel covers.

"I wish I had my camera." Angie stretched her neck to watch the begging children.

"You'll have many more opportunities to photograph this country." Ward didn't look up from his writing.

"But every road is different. Every corner brings more street children, more hungry orphans. The only constant is the desperate look in their eyes. I had that feeling when my parents died. I understand it."

"I know, my dear. Sadly, you'll see this scene duplicated in Mombasa." He squeezed her hand. "Let's catch our plane, enjoy our one-hour flight, take care of our business, and keep moving. The money we pour into this country helps the economy. It makes a difference."

Angie watched people scrounging for food as they passed a garbage dump. "But is it enough?"

Chapter Three

"Yes!" Tanner made a fist and jerked it down. "I'm going to Africa." He grabbed a canvas duffle bag out of his closet, plopped it onto his bed, unzipped it, and tossed in T-shirts, shorts, swimming trunks, and sandals.

"Hey man, what's up?" Dylan looked up from his computer screen.

"I got a call from Joseph, Alexander Ward's assistant. There's a ticket waiting for me at the airport. Ward wants me to meet him in Mombasa, Kenya, ASAP. He said something about seeing some property he's buying and walking through the mining process with him." He added some dress shirts, a sports jacket, socks, and boots.

"Sounds like fun. You've almost completed a degree giving you mining expertise, so I'm sure you'll enjoy it. My guess is Angie's there too." Dylan closed his laptop.

Tanner stuffed some jeans into his bag and carefully folded a suit and dress shirt. "Yes." He packed his shaving kit and a pair of dress shoes. "Listen, you've got a fiancé swooning at your feet, so don't give me grief about being around Angie." He put his watch on. "How about a ride to the airport?"

"Sure. When do you return?"

Tanner looked at his phone. "Monday next week, around two."

"I can get you there, but I'll park your Hummer in the garage for you before you come back since I have plans with the family. Wedding stuff. I'll text you the parking info." Dylan pointed to the bar. "It's important to make a good impression. Don't forget your sunglasses and hat so you can look the part, Indiana Jones." Dylan flipped his keys around his finger while he waited for Tanner.

After checking the date on his passport, Tanner put it in the zipper compartment of his backpack with his journal, a book, and a New Testament.

"You say you're just friends, but you're packing a bag so fast I'm getting windburn."

"Look, I've got to hurry or I'll miss my plane. Can we go?" Tanner zipped his duffle bag, slung his backpack over his shoulder, and opened the door.

Dylan hurried past him.

To Angie, Mombasa looked like Nairobi except for the palm trees and salty humidity. She soaked in the scenery as their van maneuvered through bumper-to-bumper chaos. They passed a wooden cart loaded with pineapples being pulled toward an open market by a frail man bent under its weight. A herd of cows wandered into the traffic flow. A young Masai boy used a thin switch to keep them under control, apparently losing his battle. Donkeys braying in the distance added their opinion to the cowbell serenade.

After several kilometers of potholes, they made two right

turns in the downtown area before arriving in front of the land office.

"Please wait for us, Anthony. We'll only be a few minutes." Ward led the way into the building and approached the receptionist. "I'm Alexander Ward. Vice President Saitoti sent a notification stating we would be requesting a survey of a property. Do you have those documents prepared?"

The attractive Kenyan woman behind the desk listened to his request. "Yes, sir. Give me a moment to retrieve the survey. Please take a seat."

Ward chose to stand after perusing the seating area, and Angie agreed without saying a word. The setting was very brown—brown walls and brown chairs, with brown-skinned people wearing brown uniforms. Without a breeze, the air was warm and dusty from traffic, stirring the elements and sending particles in their direction. Angie surveyed the office, the rotary phone, the carbon paper, and the bulky, worn file folders used for official transactions. Stacks of ledger books and the absence of a computer dated the establishment.

"Bwana Ward. I have the survey you have requested." The woman held a tattered folder toward him.

He stepped forward, took the file, and thanked her. "When we return with these documents, we'll need to finalize our acquisition of the property."

When the receptionist displayed questions on her countenance, not understanding his phrasing, Angie stepped forward. "We are coming back in two days to buy the land."

The woman smiled. "Enjoy your afternoon in Mombasa."

Her grand-papa led Angie to their waiting van. "You did well in there, Angelica." Ward opened the door and let Angie slip in.

"Thanks. We and the Kenyans use English but sometimes

not the same words." Angie fastened her seatbelt and came face-to-face with several dirty street children staring at her through the window. "Bwana, why are these children on the streets?"

Their driver turned toward her as he eased out of their parking place. "Their mamas and dads have died of skins disease. You call it AIDS. These children are called '*chokora*,' which means 'chicken scratching in the dirt.'" He returned his focus to the road.

"But bwana, they look hungry and scared." She kept watching until they were out of sight.

"They learn to beg, but if you give them money, they will probably buy glue with it. They sniff the glue to keep fear and hunger from consuming them." Anthony put the van in first gear and maneuvered around a pothole.

Grand-Papa patted her hand. "Angelica, we will look into their plight before we leave Kenya. Don't concern yourself."

"I don't remember there being so many orphans when we were here before." Angie sat back and hung on to the armrest for another jolt.

"AIDS has swept the country since then, and the Covid pandemic added to the number of orphans on the street." Ward opened the file about the land and flipped pages, leaving Angie with her thoughts as she stared out her window. "I'm going to do something substantial for these orphans one day, Grand-Papa."

Memories of her time in Kenya with Nana Joy helped her shelve the orphan dilemma for a while and brought a smile when they passed displays of flowers for sale. "Nana bought plants from these vendors on our last visit."

Ward reached over and patted her hand as if he remembered.

Seeing the Paradise Inn sign thrilled her. "Look, Grand-

Papa. We're here." She leaned forward as they passed the gate. "I'm glad to be back."

Ward thanked Anthony and gave him their schedule before leaving the vehicle. Wellington, their faithful employee, greeted them with a smile resembling a picket fence missing a few boards.

"Welcome back, bwana. It is good to see you, Miss Angeleeka. Your rooms are ready. Paradise Inn has missed the Wards." The old gentleman shuffled to their luggage.

"Thank you, Wellington. It is good to be here." Ward retrieved his briefcase. "Is Paul here to assist?"

"Coming, bwana. I closed the gate." Paul grabbed the two largest pieces of luggage. "Follow me, Miss Angeleeka. I will show you the way. Your room by the pool is our best one."

Bird-of-paradise flowers bloomed in front of fuchsia bougainvillea around the pool area. Palms swayed with an ocean breeze, fanning the scent of sea salt and chlorine in Angie's direction as the sound of soul-soothing waves slapped the shore. While they walked the cobblestone path back to her bungalow, the pool sparkled like a beacon, and the sun's glare warmed her skin.

"Thank you, Paul. This is nice." The suite had a sitting area and a window air conditioner cooling the space. A mosquito net hung at the head of the bed. Bottled water was provided to use for brushing her teeth. Decorated with an island theme, the place was inviting.

"Lunch will be served soon," Paul said before he left quietly.

Angie donned a bathing suit with a white sundress over it for lunch so she could lay by the pool for most of the afternoon. The shade from the palms kept the sun from burning her skin as a salty breeze cooled the sultry day. The end of October represented the beginning of summer for Kenya as opposed to the crisp, chilly temps of fall in the States.

"A soda, Miss Angeeleka?" Paul said, waiting by her side.

"That would be great. A Coke with ice, please. Paul, you still filter the water you use for the ice, don't you?"

"Absolutely." He left to serve her.

"Enjoying your afternoon?" Alexander Ward eased into the chaise lounge beside her, balancing a cup of tea.

Angie moved her sunglasses to the top of her head. "I am. It's a slice of paradise."

"I'm glad. Your grandmother loved it here. The bird-of-paradise was her favorite flower, and the lovebirds in the acacia trees kept her entertained for hours." He finished his drink. "What a lovely seascape. Remember, we're on the equator. The sun is ten times hotter, meaning you'll burn faster."

Paul returned and poured Angie's drink.

"Thanks." She took a long drink, then turned to her grandfather. "Don't worry, I came prepared. I'll protect my skin." She stirred the ice in her glass, cooling the soda. "Did you make your business calls?"

"Yes. Mason can handle the stateside mines. He's quite capable."

"That's good. Your focus needs to be here this week." Angie stroked the condensation on the outside of her glass.

"He'd like to work internationally, but I've kept him focused on local projects. I know he's frustrated, but I like to keep my eye on our foreign investments." He stood and picked up his empty cup.

"Grand-Papa, you're the boss, and Mason Malone may need to be reminded of his place at Ward Enterprises. He's a bit arrogant for my taste. His pursuit of me is a waste of time."

He laughed. "Well said." He paused. "Mason has expressed his desire to court you."

"Court me? I'm not Scarlett in *Gone With the Wind*. It's the twentieth century, for crying out loud."

Ward laughed again and shook his head.

"What?"

"You sounded like me just then. The Ward blood fills your veins." He headed toward his office suite.

Angie smiled as she watched him walk away. "Blood is thicker than water. I promise to make you proud one day." She raised her voice so he could hear her.

He laughed. "I have no doubt, Angelica. You've already made me proud." He waved and kept walking.

After a quick shower to rid her skin of sunscreen, Angie grabbed her camera and walked the beach as the sun slipped behind the horizon. Calculating the time difference, she realized that sunset would mark Tanner's arrival at the estate in Dallas. "He's there, and I'm ten thousand miles away. Maybe it's better this way. Hiding the shift in my feelings toward him would be hard." But only the sand crabs heard her as she strolled along the edge of the waves.

An ibis cawed as it flew in front of the orange sherbet-colored sunset, giving Angie a perfect panorama to bring her focus back to her photography hobby. She captured the scene with her Nikon. The sounds of waves lapping the shore and the feel of sand under her feet brought a sigh to her lips. The evening breeze caused the palm trees to waltz. It was good to be back at Paradise Inn. It was good to be out of the paparazzi's sites. She could finally relax.

The smell of grilled meat drew her to the restaurant as her grandfather made his way from the upstairs office. She took his photo and checked her screen. "You sure are handsome when you smile, Grand-Papa."

"You make me smile, my dear." He pulled out a chair for her at the table. "You love the inn, don't you?"

"Yes, it's so peaceful." Angie ordered a soda as Wellington placed a basket of bread on their table. "So when do we visit the land we're purchasing?"

"The surveyors can't meet us until the day after tomorrow. Let's rest another day. I have a few emails to answer, and taking a breather is always a good idea."

"Perfect." Angie yawned. "Sorry. I know it's not ladylike to yawn in public, but jet lag is catching up with me." She leaned back for Paul to deliver her soup. "Is it nine hours' difference right now?"

"Yes, until the time change—then it's eight hours." He reached for a roll.

She added salt to her soup as Wellington delivered her soda. "Who's going to take the lead on this tanzanite mine?"

He added white pepper to his soup. "I have some candidates in mind, but I haven't made the final decision. It's a great opportunity for someone with integrity and ambition."

"Well, good luck with that." She smiled and patted his hand, mocking his loving gesture.

Tanner enjoyed the first-class seat, the preferential treatment, and the great food. But the coddling ended once he stepped off the plane in Nairobi. He literally held his breath while he waited in the Visa line. Not in anticipation, but because of the offensive body odors of other travelers in the cue. The foods they consumed, coupled with a lack of bathing practices, caused unusual aromas to fill the small, warm area. Adding in an alcohol smell from fair-skinned tourists who indulged on the flight, the place was pungent.

Once he left the visa office, he welcomed the chaos of the baggage claim process. The baggage claim was a large warehouse-type room with low-hanging fans. Luggage belts ringed the space, delivering bags of all shapes and sizes, from expensive designer pieces to taped cardboard boxes. With thousands of travelers landing each night, the process required Job's patience.

Nairobi traffic would test even demolition derby driver's skills. His taxi driver drove him from the international airport to Wilson Airport so he could catch his flight to Mombasa. Pure mayhem ensued when too many cars took the roundabouts at the same time. Two-lane streets became four lanes with *piki pikis*, old motorcycles carrying two to four passengers and rushing between the cars and vans. Potholes added to the challenge, along with policemen directing traffic—officers who didn't know how to drive.

"We're here. Two thousand shillings, please." The driver put Tanner's duffle bag on the sidewalk. "Enjoy Mombasa." He held out his hand for payment.

Tanner placed the shillings in his hand with a generous tip. Braving the nerve-racking traffic was worth more than he could afford.

"Thanks for the ride. I'll never forget it." The drive would be forever imprinted in his memory bank in the life-threatening category. The short flight to the coast gave him time to think. To plan. He smiled as he anticipated the surprise on Angie's face when he showed up.

The plane bounced a couple of times as its wheels touched the tarmac. Palm trees in the distance marked the tropical setting. The humidity hit him as he exited the plane into Mombasa.

~

Angie enjoyed her day of swimming, sunbathing, and relaxing under swaying palms and an acacia tree with a pair of lovebirds building a nest in its branches. She donned a flowy yellow sundress for dinner and pulled her hair back with one of Nana Joy's clips. After adding a touch of lip gloss, she made her way toward the dinner table but heard voices in the lobby. Walking in that direction, she met her grandfather and Tanner. *Tanner?*

"What are you doing here?" She smiled as she grabbed his arm.

"Your grandfather—"

"I insisted he join us for these business transactions," Ward said. "It'll be a good study for him, considering his thesis topic." Ward turned to Tanner. "I trust your flights were comfortable."

"Yes, sir. I love first class. It's the only way to fly."

"Yes, it is. Now, let's have dinner and plan tomorrow's schedule." He turned toward the table in the open-air section of the small restaurant. Linen tablecloths moved with the breeze, but the bird-of-paradise flowers in the centerpiece withstood the wind.

Tanner walked to Angie's side and gave her a hug. "I couldn't let you have all the fun, could I? And don't we usually spend fall break together, Ang?"

"I didn't expect to see you here. This is Africa. You know that, right?"

"Actually, the stamp on my passport says Kenya."

"Detail, details." Hating to leave Tanner's embrace, she took her seat next to her grandfather. "Let's eat. I'm starved."

"I'm hungry too. I burned a lot of calories swimming across the ocean."

Wellington and Paul served them grilled chicken of the

skinny variety with roasted potatoes and vegetables, bread, and iced tea. Ward blessed the food.

"I'm sure your first-class ticket put you in the lap of luxury, Zarello." Angie reached for a piece of bread. "And the only water on you when you arrived was perspiration," she teased.

"It is warm here. Look, the butter is almost liquid." Tanner spread some on his bread.

"Welcome to Kenya," Ward said as he reached for the salt. "I hope you enjoy your short stay."

"Thank you, sir. I appreciate this opportunity."

Angie took a bite of her potatoes. "Grand-Papa, what time do we see the land tomorrow?"

"The surveyor can meet us at the site at nine-thirty. Let's leave here after breakfast. We'll complete the land purchase at eleven." Ward cut his vegetables. "Tanner, I have some documents you can peruse in the morning. Jet lag should have you awake early. We're purchasing a piece of property with a tanzanite mine on it. We will file the mining permit in Nairobi when we complete our work here in Mombasa."

Tanner cut his chicken. "Sounds great, sir."

"I'll leave the documents on a table in the restaurant for you. An extra set of eyes is always a good idea." Ward put the bite in his mouth. "Superb."

"Tanner, high tide is up now, but meet me on the beach when the sun rises around five-thirty. The Indian Ocean leaves amazing shells when it recedes," Angie said before she took her last bite of chicken.

"Sounds like fun." Tanner took a bite and looked around. "Wow, this is a wonderful place, Mr. Ward. Can't wait to see it in the daylight."

"It's nice. We've enjoyed it over the years—made a lot of memories." Ward continued reminiscing about happy times when Joy was at the inn as they finished dinner. He stood.

"Please tell Paul I will have my dessert and hot tea in my suite. I have an email to answer. See you two at breakfast. Get some rest. We have work to do."

Angie stood and kissed her grandfather on the cheek. "I'll talk to Paul." She went to the kitchen and returned with two pieces of pie. "When my grandfather thinks about Nana Joy, he usually draws away from people to be alone."

"That's understandable. It's hard for you too, Angie. I'm sorry." Tanner accepted the pie.

She took a deep breath and blew it out, shaking off her grief. "You want coffee or tea? Kenya has the best of both." She took her seat. "Have you tried chai? It's hot tea with hot milk and sugar—a favorite here."

"Sounds good. I'll give it a shot." Tanner yawned. "Sorry. It was a long trip."

"Two chai, Paul," Angie replied to their soft-spoken employee's inquiry.

"*Sawa, dada.* Okay, miss." Paul hurried away.

"You're right. We're ten thousand miles from Dallas, and it takes twenty-four hours to get here, but it's worth it. The scenery, the people, the food, and the animals. It will capture your heart." Angie spoke as she leaned back for Paul to serve her chai.

"So you think my heart is easy to capture? Is that what you're saying?" Tanner stirred some sugar into his tea.

"No, your heart is a treasure much to be desired. I'm talking about Kenya. You love different cultures and traveling. You can have that here—all rolled into one big adventure." She sipped her tea and held her cup as if warming her hands. "I can't believe you're here. I'm happy but shocked. You could've let me know you were coming. I felt bad about not being home for our fall break escapades." Angie took a bite of the pie.

"But I didn't know until it was almost time to go to the

airport, and I couldn't exactly call your cell." He tasted his chai. "I like it. Is the pie good?"

"Yep, really good. Remember your manners. Your mother taught you not to lick your plate." She smiled and took another bite.

"Yes, she did. I was eight at the time."

Angie laughed. "I think I saw you do it when you were fifteen."

"I think you know too much about me, Ang."

She laughed.

Wet sand oozed between Angie's toes as she strolled the beach. She'd collected a queen conch shell and several sand dollars before Tanner arrived.

"Now this is a seascape. It's breathtaking." He stood with his hands in the pockets of his shorts, his tank top revealing muscular shoulders and a deep tan.

Angie focused on his espresso-colored eyes, long black eyelashes, and the lock of black hair falling across his forehead. "Words can't describe it. You have to walk the shore, feel the breeze, and hear the waves to get the full effect."

Three Kenyans passed in a dug-out canoe, handfishing for their breakfast—a startling contrast to the expensive catamaran gliding across the horizon. Palm trees swayed in the breeze. A few iridescent crabs scampered away, ducking into holes in the sand. Ibis soaring above them cawed. Tanner pivoted, taking in his surroundings.

"You're right. It's indescribable. I love it." Tanner put his hand over his eyes to shade them from the sun's glare.

"I knew you would. Let's see what shells we can find." She picked up a shell. "Here's a knobbed whelk. It's been abandoned by a crab who moved on to a bigger house." Angie added it to her collection.

"Just like we do. We have to keep up with the Joneses." He squatted on the sand and dug out two half-buried shells. "Here are a couple of shells abandoned by some clams." He showed her his find.

"I don't understand what the Joneses have to do with shells."

"No, I guess you wouldn't. Middle-class Americans continually increase the model of their car or the size of their house to outdo their neighbors. It's an unspoken competition."

"But, why does that matter? Shouldn't they just do their best without the pressure of competing?"

"They should. It's just part of our culture." He moved closer to the waves. "Your clamshell is called the common limpet."

"I didn't know you knew so much about seashells."

"Only this one. We discected one in biology that some guy brought to class." He washed his hands in the waves.

"Let's get a box from the kitchen to carry our treasures. Look at these. I love these long white ones. They resemble angel wings." She dusted sand off the shells.

"Are there any starfish?" Tanner picked up some smaller specimens.

Angie struggled to open a clam. "I haven't seen any on this trip. Right now, I'm looking for a pearl. I've found a few, but they're small. Sometimes I find some beautiful coral, since there's a coral reef about fifty yards out. That's why the waves are small, and it keeps the sharks away from the shallow water."

"For a pretty rich girl, you're really smart." He smiled and kept gathering shells.

"Are you saying I'm pretty or I'm pretty rich?" She put her hands on her hips and faced him.

"Well, I think you're both. I'll get a box for your keepsakes." He hurried toward the resort.

Angie stood statuesque, replaying his words. She edged into the surf, allowing its coolness to wash over her feet as she strategized her next move. Rubbing elbows with her hunky friend in a foreign country offered her a wealth of opportunities, but she'd guard their friendship. True friends were scarce in her world. *But what do I do when my heartbeat escalates with every whiff of his masculine scent?*

Ward checked his watch. "Our ride should be here in thirty minutes. We'll visit the property first. Tanner, let's check the fencing and the strength of the gate. We must consider the security of our team. Angelica, have the surveyor show you the boundary markers. They may be outside the fenced area." Ward sipped the last of his tea.

"I think you're correct about the markers," Tanner said. "The small survey in the documents shows them at a strange angle. Their boundaries aren't exactly straight." He showed Ward an example on the survey.

"Good eye, Tanner," Angie said, leaning toward her grandfather to look over his shoulder. "What about the ocean side of the property? Is it secured with fencing?"

"I'm not sure. Tanner, check that side too." Ward stood. "After you finish, I want us to sketch the mining platform we need to have built. We must keep this mine under wraps for security reasons. I have a builder I can trust with the project. He built Paradise Inn." Ward stood. "Let's be ready to leave in ten. I'm going to show our driver this map."

"We better get a move on, Zarello. You've got to earn your keep. You can only get so far on your good looks." Angie smirked and headed to her bungalow. "I know what you've been doing. You've sweet-talked your professors to get that four-point-O."

"You probably paid for yours." He laughed out loud.

Winding dirt roads led them to the property. A rickety fence clung to a strong gate, rusted from the salty air. Patches of tall grass bent with the ocean breeze. A nest of storks was the only sign of life in the small rainforest camouflaging the location of the mine.

When the dust settled, Angie stepped out of their taxi. "Not your finest piece of property, Grand-Papa."

"But probably the most valuable." Ward greeted the surveyor, who approached with rolls of plans to assist in their assessment of the land.

"I'm starting on the beachfront area of the property," Angie said, leaving the men to scan the white paper spread out on the hood of the taxi.

"Watch where you step, Angie. There's a large hole in the ground by the marker on the right," Tanner called out as she walked away.

"I'll be careful. No falling for me." *Not that kind of falling.*

Chapter Four

Trees and scrub brush hid the spot where the mining platform would be constructed. Palm trees offered the only reprieve as the tropical sun glared down on Angie's unprotected skin. Her flowy sundress moved with the breeze. Having completed her assignment, she held the measuring tape for Tanner as he and Grand-Papa drew a diagram for the platform.

"Grand-Papa, will this be generator-run? I don't see any power lines." Angie popped the release on the tape measure.

"Yes, a smaller platform will be built several feet away from the mine for the generator and fuel supply to keep the fumes and noise level away from the employees." Ward walked past the mine to a level area. "Tanner, let's put a covered workbench here for the gemologist to utilize."

"I'll make a note of it, sir." He wrote something on a tablet.

"And make sure the cords on their tools reach the generator." Ward scanned the area. "Work on this layout while we eat, Tanner. It may need adjusting." He looked around the property and started for the taxi. "Our work is done here. Let's have lunch."

Angie matched his stride. "Is it a good purchase, Grand-Papa?"

He opened the door for Angie and Tanner to get in. "Absolutely. One of my best." Ward instructed Anthony to drive them to a Kenyan hotel twenty minutes from the property.

"Angelica, I'll order lunch. Will you ask to see the rooms? They need to be self-contained, meaning each one has a bathroom. This would be a good place for the team to stay while working at the mine." Ward spoke as they parked in front of a hotel.

"Sure, glad to." She pulled a tablet and pen out of her bag.

"Tanner, let's peruse the documents again before we sign the land deal and make the final payment."

"No problem. I've been thinking about the housing for the generator. I want to discuss it with the builder and ask specific questions concerning the pulley system they recommend to lower those mining the stones."

"That's why I had you join us. I'll get him on the phone while we're at lunch."

After an extended call with the builder, Ward ordered the materials to have the perimeter fence constructed and the mining structure built. Within four hours, they had secured the property and the housing for the team and finalized plans with the builder.

As Anthony drove them back to the inn, Ward gave Angie and Tanner their schedule. "A good day's work, you two. You can relax this afternoon. During dinner, we'll plan our work in Nairobi. We'll complete the purchase of this property before we fly out in the morning." Ward exited the vehicle and ordered a soft drink from Wellington, who greeted them upon arrival.

"I'm going to cool off in the pool. What about you,

Tanner?" Angie grabbed her bag and headed toward her bungalow.

"Why swim in a pool when you have an ocean calling your name?" When he passed the kitchen, Tanner asked for a bottle of cold water to drink as he changed into his swimming trunks.

"Yeah, I hear the waves saying 'Lazy bum, lazy bum.'" She laughed.

He cupped his hand around his ear. "Well, that's better than 'Prima donna, prima donna.'"

"Oh, you're so funny. Ha, ha."

"Okay, let's swim in the ocean first, then the pool. That work for you?" He guzzled some of the water.

"Yep."

This was a mistake. Seeing Angie's perfect curves in a blue two-piece and her jet-black hair blowing in the breeze knocked the wind out of Tanner. At this rate, he wouldn't have to hold his breath when he swam. Her deep-blue eyes sparkled when she smiled, challenging him to a race before she plunged into the saltwater and gained a head start. Maybe the cold water would bring his mind under control.

"I win, slowpoke." Angie pushed the hair out of her eyes and treaded water until he reached her. "You may look strong, but you just lost to a girl."

"Cheater. You won awards in swim racing." He continued to tread water. "At least I didn't have to save your life this time."

"Well, there's that." She put her hand on his head and pushed him under.

Tanner grabbed her leg and pulled her beneath the surface. The silky feel of her skin caught him off guard. She was beautiful, no longer the awkward preteen taking dance lessons. He was drawn to this version of Angie like gravity. It was time to return to shore.

Angie came up, spitting saltwater.

"The last one to the pool serves the Cokes." He took off and beat her to the pool. "I want ice in my glass, and bring a snack, will ya?" he said when he came up from the water. He splashed her before she could speak. "And I need a towel."

"Anything else, oh king of beasts?" She bowed.

"No, that will be all. And chop, chop." He dove again, cutting off any response.

When she returned with a tray, he pushed himself up on the side of the pool and grabbed the towel she offered. Taking a lounge chair, he reclined as she bent forward to pour his soda. This view of her body sent warm feelings through him—until she purposely dropped ice in his lap. "You're ... you're ..." He searched for the right word.

"Lovely, kind, smart, intelligent?" She smirked.

"Unforgettable."

"Really? What do you mean by that?" She sat in the chair beside him.

"It's a secret. If I tell you, I'll have to kill you." He flopped his shades onto his eyes, grabbed a French fry, and dipped it in ketchup.

Angie finished her black currant soda and clinked the ice cubes in her glass. Unforgettable ... what did that mean? Was he saying she was a dream come true or a nightmare that wouldn't end? He wouldn't give her a straight answer. Instead, he hid behind sarcasm and offered such quick comebacks she could hardly keep up.

She opened her sunscreen and rubbed some on her legs and arms, trying to ignore the hunky hero reclining in the next chair. She flipped through a magazine she'd picked up at the airport and attempted to control her focus.

"Enjoying that magazine?"

"Yes. Why do you ask?"

"It's upside-down." He leaned forward, raised his shades, and grinned.

She turned it around and started at the beginning again. "I wanted to see if you'd notice."

"Yeah, right." He lowered his shades and relaxed. "Ang ... can I ask you something?"

"Sure."

"Do the paparazzi incidents still bother you?" He sat up and put his hands on his knees.

Meeting his gaze, she lifted her sunglasses. "It's been great to relax and not think about it while I've been in Kenya, but it does bother me. I try to bury my anxiety and put on a happy face. But I dream about drowning when I sleep, and thoughts of the photographer invading my space make me nervous— jumpy at sudden noises during the day."

He took her hand. "I'm sorry. I wish I could fix it for you."

"Being there for me has meant a lot. I'm asking the Lord for peace."

"And He's the giver of peace. I'm praying for you every day."

"Thanks, Tanner." She put her sunglasses back on but didn't let his hand go.

Paul loaded their bags into the van and opened the sliding door for Angie. Tanner waited until Alexander Ward had taken his seat before climbing in. Potholes, exhaust fumes, and roundabouts made for quite the adventurous trek through Mombasa, but Tanner enjoyed the ride.

"It was dark when I came through here last time," he said. "Exciting place. I love the huge tusks built across the road." He took a picture with his phone.

"Mombasa is a great place to visit," Angie said. "You can't drink the water, and you have to watch your back, but it sure takes me back when I see meat hanging in the butcher shops, fruit and vegetables being sold on the streets, and the animals roaming freely between the cars. You know you're in Africa when you see hawkers selling mangos, soccer balls, and calendars along the road. And the sweet-spirited people make it a paradise. It's awesome."

"Well said, my dear." Ward leaned forward and pointed to the building they needed. "Now, to purchase the property. Follow me."

The banker and his guard waited inside the office to receive the check for the property once the deed had been signed and transferred. The process resembled transactions in the States except for the constant need for carbon paper to duplicate the documents. Tanner found their antiquated methods interesting to watch. Ward stood, took the deed, and shook hands with the real estate officer before giving the check to the banker.

Once back in the van, Angie broke the silence. "Grand-Papa, how did you learn the process of acquiring land in Kenya?"

"When I bought the acreage for Paradise Inn, Paul walked me through it, explaining the steps and protocols."

"It was good to see it in action. Thanks for letting Angie and me join you," Tanner said as he watched the traffic.

"No problem." Ward glanced at the scenery as they neared the airport.

"Tanner, we're almost at the airport. Can you handle the luggage while I get us checked in?"

"I can, sir."

The morning passed in a flurry. The flight from the coast was bumpy, with turbulent storm clouds gathering, ready to soak the earth at any moment. Once in Nairobi, Martin met them for their short ride to the office to file for their mining permit and expedited their task. Any moments gained were lost as the secretaries moved in slow motion, using carbon paper and clear Bic pens to fill out several documents.

Enduring the lack of air conditioning, Angie fanned herself to keep the Kenyans' body odor at bay and pesky flies from landing on her face. Maintaining her professional posture, she listened as her grandfather patiently negotiated the deal with the man in charge.

Tanner stood at his side, watching and listening to the conversation.

With the mining permit acquired, they left the office and breathed in a mixture of dust, exhaust, and sunshine.

"Let's have lunch, shall we?" Ward led the way to meet Martin, who waited by their van. "Giraffe Manor on Koitobos Road, bwana." Ward relaxed against the bench seat.

"Really, Grand-Papa?" Angie reached for her bag.

"I thought you'd enjoy it, Angelica."

"What's Giraffe Manor?" Tanner asked.

"Here it is." She began to read from her magazine featuring Kenyan articles and information. *"Giraffe Manor is located on one hundred and forty acres of indigenous forest, where a herd of*

Rothschild's giraffes roam freely. The manor is modeled after a Scottish hunting lodge and is an experience of a lifetime." She hugged her grandfather. "This will be great."

"This lodge has wonderful food. You'll enjoy it. After we eat, I have a couple meetings to plan. You two have fun. Get some good pictures. Martin will take you to visit the baby elephants after you feed the giraffe. When you return, we'll have hors d'oeuvres with the giraffe stealing off our plates then enjoy a quiet dinner in the main dining room."

"Sounds like fun." Tanner grinned.

Tanner took a great shot of Angie feeding a giraffe, then one of her hugging it, catching her pretty face in the photo. The sun glistened on her black hair as a gentle wind tossed it about. Her burgundy lips and deep-blue eyes glowed in the sunlight.

"Here, Tanner. Hold one of these pellets in your mouth, and she'll come take it from you."

"You're kidding, right?"

"Nope. Try it. I'll have my camera ready." She snapped the picture at the exact moment the giraffe grabbed the pellet and licked Tanner's jaw with her eighteen-inch, slimy black tongue.

"Gross! You knew what was going to happen!" He turned on Angie, wiping saliva from his jaw.

Angie was laughing so hard she couldn't speak. Doubling over, she held her stomach. "It ... it was a perfect shot of you kissing a girl in Kenya. It'll go viral on Twitter. You'll be famous. I can see it now—Tanner Zarello—Ladies Man!"

"Oh, you're so funny." He used his sleeve to wipe his mouth, then eased closer to her. With an evil look in his eyes, he grabbed her and wiped his slimy cheek on her shoulder.

"Don't, Tanner!"

He laughed. Angie squirmed and let out a squeal. The female giraffe bumped Tanner's back, pushing him face-to-face with Angie. He grabbed her to keep from falling, and his laughter died as he stared into her eyes. The feel of her skin messed with his control. Her breath warmed his face. Her soft lips were inches from his. Caught in the moment, he froze. Her hands were on his chest. He sucked in a breath, released her, and stepped back.

Angie stared, speechless. "Tanner ... say something."

He paused. Searched for words. "Elephants. We need to see the elephants."

Angie felt sparks from Tanner's touch and didn't want it to end. If she read the look in his eyes correctly, Tanner felt it too. The fireworks between them were palpable. She wanted him to talk about the elephant in the room, but he didn't. Maybe he really would rather visit some pachyderms than gamble with their friendship.

The VIP passes the vice president left at the gate for them gave Tanner and Angie special privileges regular guests weren't allowed to enjoy.

"Miss Ward, we have a newborn elephant whose mother was killed for her tusks. He is now hungry. Do you want to feed him his bottle?" the tour guide asked.

"I'd love to. Tanner, take my picture." Angie gave him her camera and followed the handler into a stall. "Look how sweet he is." Angie eased closer. The baby reached for her with his trunk. Angie grinned and rubbed his head.

Tanner moved from one vantage point to another, taking photos. "Look this way, Angie." He took a shot just as the pachyderm wrapped his trunk around her neck and pulled her close. "He's flirting with you, Ang."

"His name is Mukkoka. He is eleven months old. We found him wandering alone by the Kiva River in Tsavo. Here's his bottle. You have to coax him to take it, but once he realizes it's milk, it will vanish just like that." The handler snapped his fingers for emphasis.

Angie offered the baby elephant the bottle. "Come on. Try this. You'll like it." On her third try, the infant accepted her offering. A loud sucking noise filled the stall as milk dripped onto Angie's shoes. "Look, Tanner. He likes it." She looked up and grinned, giving him the perfect photo op.

The elephant finished the bottle in no time. Angie held up the empty container. "I think he's still hungry."

"But we must feed him in increments. His stomach is not large yet." The handler took the bottle and led them to the outside pen. The baby elephant followed Angie to the gate.

"Bwana, would you like to help with the bigger babies? I have some rubber boots and a jumpsuit for you in the office." The handler led the way.

Angie took the camera from Tanner. "Do it. It'll be fun."

"Sure, I'm game. I'm going to change. I'll be right back." Tanner followed the handler.

The manager of the facility greeted Tanner. "Welcome to Sheldricks. Our boots and jumpsuits are in this adjacent room."

"Can I ask you a question? How do you adopt an elephant?"

He smiled and handed him a clipboard. "Fill this out and give me five thousand shillings."

Tanner took the clipboard and offered the shillings. "I want to adopt Mukkoka."

"I will give you a packet of information and a certificate before you leave." He pointed toward the boots and jumpsuits.

"Let's keep this between us, okay?"

"No problem, bwana."

Tanner changed into the boots, zipped the jumpsuit, and followed the employee into a large empty pen. Wheelbarrows with large bottles of goat milk were ready for consumption. Water troughs were full and mud holes were being sprayed by workers for pachyderm playtime.

He heard the youngsters trumpeting as their handlers led them to the observation area. Tanner was surrounded in no time, holding two bottles as he dodged mud slung by a feisty Dumbo a few feet away.

Angie put her camera to good use. Close-ups of baby elephants were rare, but with their mothers out of the picture, her photos would be worthy of National Geographic. Tanner started to feed another young elephant just as the mud-bath queen decided she liked the good-looking American. She left the mud puddle and slung mud toward Tanner.

"Tanner!" He looked at Angie just as mud splattered his face. Angie caught the action and giggled at his expression. "It looks good on you!"

One of the handlers gave him a rag. He wiped his face, smearing the sticky mud. Tourists watching the scene laughed and captured pictures on their cell phones. Tanner smiled at Angie and bowed to the gathering onlookers, taking it in stride.

After Tanner returned the boots and jumpsuit and spent

some time with a water hose, they returned to their van for their trek to Giraffe Manor.

Angie slipped out of the vehicle and faced Tanner. "I had fun, and you were a good sport, Zarello."

"Have you already posted the photo across cyberspace?"

"Not on Twitter yet, but your mother loved the giraffe kiss and the mud facial. The whole staff has probably seen it by now." She laughed.

Tanner smiled. "This is a face only a mother could love." He patted his cheeks.

Angie entered the manor to change for dinner. "I don't know. The jury is still out on that one."

From the mouth of the judge …

As they sat on the second floor of the hotel for breakfast, a giraffe watched them curiously through the window. When a basket of toast was placed on the table, the very tall intruder stuck his head through the window and stole some toast with his long, slimy tongue. A uniform-clad waiter stood by their table, prepared to bring more.

"Bwana, you knew he was going to steal our toast?" Angie asked.

"It is his favorite, so we prepare extra." He replaced their toast and removed the empty basket. "I have placed buckets of pellets on the floor by your table. Offer the bucket when your food arrives if you plan to eat your meal." He smiled and returned to the kitchen.

"The look on your face is priceless." Tanner showed his phone screen to Grand-Papa. "I'm posting this. It may end your paparazzi problem."

"Oh, you're so funny. Let me see it." Angie reached for his

phone, but he pressed send before he let her see the picture. "That's a horrible photo."

"I love the long, slimy black tongue in front of your face." He laughed. "So attractive. Sorta resembles a slug."

Ward chuckled at their banter. "Since we have several hours to spare, I've arranged a safari truck to pick you two up in thirty minutes to take you to Nairobi Game Park."

Angie clapped her hands. "I love safaris. Come with us, Grand-Papa." She put her hand on his arm to stop his exit.

"Reclining with a good book sounds like a great afternoon for this senior citizen. You two have fun." Ward stood and set a tip on the table.

Tanner stood in respect for Alexander Ward. "Thank you, sir."

"No problem. Angelica, get your camera."

"Meet you at the truck, Tanner." Angie left to grab her Nikon. Angie climbed into the safari vehicle and found Tanner chatting with the driver. The truck had elevated seating on three levels, giving the passengers significant access to photograph the wildlife. Its four-wheel-drive capabilities carried tourists through the rough terrain to view the wildlife. "Angie, Silas is our tour guide for today's adventure."

"Hello, Silas. Glad to meet you. Can you take me to some lions?"

"Yes, miss." Silas's smile was missing a tooth. She whispered in Tanner's ear, "Masai extract a permanent tooth so when they get lockjaw, they can still eat and drink through the empty space."

Bouncing along the park's dirt roads, they enjoyed the breeze blowing through the open-air safari truck. With downtown Nairobi in the background, they traded the smell of exhaust for animal droppings as their search for wild animals commenced.

"It'd be a shame to travel all this distance and not go on a safari." Tanner opened Angie's camera case. "You still carry those binoculars, Ang?"

"Yeah, they're in the zipper compartment. Would you hand me the longer lens, please?" Angie swapped her lens as Silas stopped in the middle of some grazing zebra and impala. "I agree, Tanner. You can't travel this far and not see the wildlife. I'm glad we could do this together."

He reached over and squeezed her shoulder. "Me too, Ang. You're my top choice for safari companions."

Their driver continued his tour-guide speech. "There's one male impala, and this is his harem. These animals feed together. *Hakuna matata.* No problem. The few zebras we have here in Nairobi have chosen to stay here and not migrate with the wildebeest. Years ago, the migration traveled this far north, but not anymore."

"Are lions nearby?" Tanner asked as he scanned the area.

"Yes, they are near, but they rest in the day and hunt and eat at night. But if you see one, do not approach, or they will have a daytime American snack." He laughed. "They might like white meat."

Easing a kilometer down the road, he slowed the truck. "You are surrounded now. Jackals are resting by that acacia tree, with mongoose playing nearby. You can see a vulture in the tall, dead tree to their right." He pointed. "There are warthogs in the weeds in front of us and elands in the distance to our left."

"Look, Tanner. Mongoose are climbing on those warthogs." Angie took several shots.

"The mongoose eat ticks off the warthogs." Silas cranked the truck.

Tanner laughed. "That's neighborly of them."

"Are the animals always this close together?" Angie focused on the elands and waited for them to turn toward her.

"No, we can drive many kilometers and see nothing at all. Not even a dung beetle."

Tanner laughed. "Angie wants a picture of a dung beetle, Silas. Can you find one?"

Angie hit Tanner's arm. "I do not. Don't listen to him."

They hit a pothole as their driver left the road to bring them closer to some waterbucks.

"Woah!" Angie laughed as she hung on to the window frame until they stopped for a photo. "Is that eucalyptus I smell?"

Their guide grabbed a leaf off a bush by the driver's-side door. "It's mint." He rubbed the leaves between his fingers. "Smell. We use it as medicine for the stomach."

Angie smelled the leaves as static from a CB radio caught the driver's attention. He spoke in Swahili for a few seconds.

"Hold on. A cheetah has been spotted. We must move."

Leaving the area, they drove across the grassy plains, around some boulders, and through a riverbed before stopping in a valley. Silas looked through his binoculars, dropped them in the passenger seat, and took off again.

"Now we're on safari. Isn't this great?" Angie hung onto her sunglasses as they bounced across the rugged terrain.

"Yeah, it's the best."

They reached the top of a knoll and saw a circle of safari vehicles.

"The mama cheetah has two cubs. You are very lucky to see her." Silas eased their truck into the circle of rubberneckers.

"Amazing." Angie quickly took a series of shots. Using his phone, Tanner took a great photo of Angie smiling with cheetahs in the background. Definitely frame-worthy.

Silas spoke to another driver, then turned back to them.

"There has been a kill. A black mane has taken a zebra. You want to go there?"

"Yes, lions are why we came," Tanner said. "Hang on, Ang. We're going on a lion hunt."

Within fifteen minutes, Silas parked the vehicle beside a fresh kill. Vultures circled overhead, and hyenas eased closer, preparing to steal the meat.

"Silas, I can see hyenas in the tall grasses to the left." She took a close-up with her strong lens.

"If you watch closely, you will find some jackals in this direction. It's the African pecking order. Lion, hyena, jackal, then the vultures will clean the bones."

Tanner recorded the scene. The sound of crunching bones filled the air. Blood spewed as the king of beasts displayed his brute strength. "Wildcat Diaries, eat your heart out. I'm getting some great footage."

"I'm glad you're enjoying all the blood and guts, Zarello."

"Ang, he's the king of the jungle. When else would I get to see nature in action like this?"

"Not often. So film away." Angie noticed movement in the bushes. She touched Tanner's shoulder and lowered her voice. "Tanner, hyenas are moving in."

He turned and caught the action on video.

Silas also watched the impending battle. "They will make the lion leave and eat their fill."

The lion lifted his head at the sound of the hyenas laughing. He growled and charged the leader of the pack but was soon surrounded. He took a few more bites of meat before he gave up the fight.

Tanner filmed the jackals waiting nearby and the vultures circling overhead before he cut the camera off. "Thanks for letting me use your camera." He gave it back to Angie.

"No problem. I'll be sure you get a copy of this footage."

She stored the camera in her bag. "There's nothing more exhilarating than taking pictures of the Lord's handiwork up close and personal." She glanced at her watch. "Silas, I hate for our fun to end, but we have to get back. My grandfather will be waiting for us. But we can safari on the way if you notice something we haven't seen today."

"*Hakuna Matata.* No problem." He drove them back in another direction, stopping briefly when he spotted a cape buffalo wallowing in a mudhole.

Spotting a ball of mistletoe—a kissing ball—in a tree beside the muddy animal, Angie took a close-up and smiled.

"Do you like cape buffalos, Ang?"

"Not normally, but I wanted that photo." She kept taking pictures in their few remaining moments in the park. A pair of ostriches strutted in the distance, with a giraffe feeding on acacia trees against the tree line. Some Thompson gazelle grazed near the road as they approached the gate.

Traffic jams, honking horns, and exhaust plagued their return to Giraffe Manor. After bidding Silas goodbye, Angie hurried to the desk for her key.

"We meet Grand-Papa here in the foyer in forty-five minutes," Angie said. "I've got to hurry." She took the stairs, not waiting for the elevator.

Tanner spoke to her retreating form. "Don't worry about me. I'll be ready."

Angie took a deep breath as they entered the gorgeous hotel ballroom. A steward took her evening jacket before leading them to one of the head tables marked RESERVED. Alexander Ward walked in front of her and Tanner. Tanner extended his arm, and Angie placed her hand in the crook of his elbow. He looked debonair in his fitted dinner jacket with an open-collared dress shirt that accentuated the muscular curves of his torso.

"You look beautiful, Ang."

"Thanks, Tanner. Every debutant must own a little black dress for such occasions. This is mine." They entered in tandem.

"Well, I like it."

"Thanks. You clean up pretty good yourself. Maybe it was yesterday's facial treatments. Did you get all the mud out of your ear?" Angie teased him quietly so the guests wouldn't overhear.

"I think I did. At least I don't smell anymore." He pulled out her chair.

"Oh, I think you smell amazing. But let's keep it a secret." She squeezed his arm, then turned and greeted those seated at their table and started a conversation with the United States ambassador's wife.

The ballroom sparkled with crystal chandeliers and shiny floors. American music played softly as important guests arrived. Massive bouquets of long-stemmed red roses were strategically placed throughout the ballroom, and flickering candles provided ambient lighting. Soon, the vice president and his family were announced. Everyone stood in their honor as they were ushered into the venue while Kenya's national anthem played.

Vice President Saitoti escorted his wife to her chair and stepped to the podium.

"Welcome, everyone. It is our delight to have you join us for this celebration. This occasion will serve as an official engagement announcement for two special people. We are honored you're in attendance." He introduced his daughter and her fiancé, their family members, and all the officials in the ballroom. "My dear friend from America is with us this evening. I'm honored to introduce Alexander Ward and his granddaughter, Angelica. Please give them greetings."

Ward and Angie stood and waved to the gathering of VIPs.

"This casual evening of celebration is not usually a part of Kenyan culture. My daughter and her fiancé have been schooled in the States, where exceptions to the rules are incorporated as a part of weddings. We hope you enjoy the evening, the food, and the beverages. After the appetizers are served, the engaged couple will have their first dance. As it comes to a close, please feel free to join them on the dance floor."

When the vice president took his seat, conversations rose around the massive room. Angie thought the evening was lovely, including the Kenyan appetizers. Tasty tarts and arrowroot chips with spicy relish provided a wonderful mixture of salty and savory. Juicy pieces of goat with a touch of barbecue sauce were served on small crackers, and prawns were offered in a flute with ketchup.

"This food is great. The goat is surprisingly tender." Tanner took another bite.

"You sound surprised." Angie filled her fork with a juicy prawn.

"I am, but pleased." He reached for a piece of bread. "I think I saw flan on the dessert trays, Ang."

"Perfect." She smiled. "Look at the couple. They're a portrait of love in motion. Aren't they beautiful together, Tanner?" Angie smiled.

"Yes, they are." Tanner watched the couple waltz. "Ready to show them how to dance?" He stood and offered Angie his hand.

"Excuse us, Grand-Papa." Angie put her hand in Tanner's.

Ward waved at Angie and continued his conversation with the ambassador.

Once on the dance floor, Angie stepped close to Tanner and placed one hand on his left shoulder and the other on his right hand. She met his eyes, signaling she was ready. He led with confidence. Their practiced waltz routine carried them across the floor like professionals.

"You're good at this. You know that?" Angie stared into his chocolate eyes.

"Yeah, and it didn't cost me a dime. I benefitted from all your dance lessons." He dipped Angie, then spun her around before drawing her close again. Their moves caught the attention of the guests.

"I think we've got an audience." Angie smiled.

"Then let's throw in a few spins, shall we?"

"Sure."

When he held her close again, he dipped her. "You're pretty good at this yourself, Miss Ward." He pulled her near.

"Nana Joy insisted I'd be a good dancer, and you were the only partner available."

"Huh, and I thought you had a crush on me."

"Nah, the crush didn't come until later—much later."

"When?"

"Tanner—"

"Yes."

"The music stopped."

Chapter Five

Because they sat in different parts of first-class and rushed through London's Heathrow Airport to catch their next flight, Tanner was never close enough to Angie to have a meaningful conversation with her until they reached customs in Dallas.

"Thank you for including me in these transactions, Mr. Ward. It was a great experience in the field of my studies. Very enlightening." Tanner grabbed Ward's suitcase and pulled it off the conveyor belt for him.

"I'm glad you could join us. I see great things in your future, Tanner." Ward, wearing a suit and a dress shirt sans the customary tie, leaned on his cane as they waited for Angie's luggage.

"I appreciate that, sir."

Angie's Louis Vuitton bag appeared on the luggage belt. Tanner stepped forward and retrieved it, then rolled it toward Angie. She reminded him of a model on a runway. Her perfect hair, makeup, clothes, and pearly-white teeth stole his breath. "S—See you on Thanksgiving Day, Ang. My truck's in the garage, and I see your limo at the curb." He lifted his duffle bag and hung it across his shoulder. "Are we doing Christmas decorations again?"

"Yep, and I'm adding a few more trees, so we'll have a lot to do." Angie rolled her bag to their driver, James.

Tanner gave Ward's suitcase to James as well. "Mr. Ward, please don't let her go overboard."

A small smile curled the corners of Ward's lips. "Son, you should know by now that when Angelica gets a plan in her pretty little head, there's no stopping her. I hope you like to climb ladders. All I can say is hang on and watch your step." He followed James to the curb.

"After you, Angie." Tanner trailed her like a shadow but reached around to open the limo door just as a photographer took her picture.

"Angie, I hear you've been to Africa," the photographer said. "Welcome back. Did you enjoy your first-class seat? Did they wine and dine you like royalty? Was a safari part of your itinerary? You plan to travel again soon?" He stepped closer and stuck a mike in her face.

Angie put her hands out in front of her. "Tanner, make him stop."

Tanner stepped between Angie and the camera, blocking his shot. He managed to usher Angie into the limo and shut the door.

"Get them home, James." He hit the top of the car as it pulled away then turned on the paparazzi, grabbing his shirt at the neckline.

"What's your name?" Tanner struggled to keep his voice down.

"Why? What's it to you?" When the photographer pulled away, his shirt stretched in Tanner's grip. "You can read my byline when I publish these photos."

"Looks like a recent wound there on your nose. Did you

break it? Are you the one who used a drone to get pics of Miss Ward at the Ward Estate? She almost drowned. That's attempted murder! Did you know that?"

"Hey, man—let go of me! Photographers have a job to do. Her front page spread will be my big break. I've been sent to get this story." He tried to jerk his shirt out of Tanner's grip.

Tanner let him go, pushing him away as a security guard approached. "Stay away from her, or I'll be pressing charges. Understand?"

He held his hands up in surrender, his camera hanging from a strap around his neck. "No harm, no foul. She's a celebrity. With wealth comes publicity. It's the name of the game, and this is my job." He straightened his shirt and stepped back.

"Clichés don't excuse an invasion of privacy and reckless endangerment. So back off. I mean it!" Tanner stood his ground.

"You got it, man." The photographer hurried toward the escalator.

Tanner took a deep breath and blew it out in a huff. *With this guy pursuing her, protecting Angie is all-encompassing. She shouldn't go out unaccompanied.* He punched Ellis's number into his phone as he walked the ramp to the parking garage.

"Ellis. Tanner here. The paparazzi showed up at the airport. If this is the same guy, he's not quite six feet tall, with shaggy brown hair, brown eyes, and acne scars on his face. I threatened him and demanded that he back off." He listened to Ellis for a moment. "Okay, I'll keep you in the loop."

Tanner drove back to the university, thinking of his run-in with the annoying photographer. *He's obsessed with Angie and displaying possessive stalker tendencies. That makes him dangerous. This is the third time he's threatened Angie.* He decided to mention the stalker possibility to Ellis and

Alexander Ward so they would strengthen their security plan.

Leaving the airport, Tanner took a deep breath and tried to shake off his angst by letting his thoughts return to Kenya. He remembered the shape of Angie's silhouette, the shine of her hair, and the sparkle of her deep-blue eyes when she laughed. She was stunning. Model material. All she needed was a runway. He understood how her wealth and beauty could easily draw stalkers like a magnet. Security had to be heightened.

Preparing for finals kept Angie busy since her return from Africa two weeks prior. She'd only seen her grandfather once since they landed. She powered down her laptop and went to the formal dining room to meet Grand-papa for dinner.

"Happy birthday, Angelica." Alexander Ward kissed one of Angie's cheeks, then the other.

"Thanks, Grand-Papa."

He pulled out her chair. "Let's have dinner. I've requested your favorites. Then we can open your gifts. A cake with twenty candles is waiting for you in the kitchen." His laugh lines crinkled next to his eyes.

"I love it when you smile." She opened her silverware wrapped in linen.

"Today, we celebrate you, my dear." He took his seat and removed the silver domes on their plates. "Ta-da!"

"Shrimp Alfredo. You better pray fast. I studied through my lunch break, and I'm starving." She tasted her Alfredo as soon as he offered thanks. "This is divine."

"Your parents were ecstatic when you were born, Angelica. It was a momentous day for all of us. Nana Joy cried the first time she held you, and a new level of happiness entered this family. Now look at you. You've grown into such a beautiful young woman. I couldn't be prouder."

"Thanks, Grand-Papa." She hugged his neck.

"I don't want to wait. Here. Open your gift from me." He handed her a small box.

She slid the ribbon off. Lifting the lid, she found a set of keys. "Keys! What did you get me?"

"A Lexus SUV, top of the line with all the bells and whistles."

Angie laughed. "I've never heard you say 'whistles.'"

"The salesman kept repeating the phrase." He laughed.

"I appreciate the generous gift. What color is it?"

"Deep blue, of course. I wanted you to have a new vehicle before you moved south to your college town." He reached for another package. "I think this one is from Tanner."

She tore into it and found a framed picture of her feeding the baby elephant, Makkoka. "Look, Grand-Papa." She showed him the photo and opened Tanner's note.

Angie, I'm proud to inform you that you've adopted an elephant.

Makkoka is yours.

Happy Birthday!

Tanner

"He adopted an elephant for me. I loved the little pachyderm. What a special gift." She looked at her grandfather and smiled. "I'll call Tanner later. Thanks for the SUV."

"You're welcome. Let's eat, have some cake, and take your Lexus for a drive."

~

Tanner pressed Angie's name on his cell and waited as it rang. "Happy Birthday, Ang. Did you get my gift?" Tanner popped the top on a Coke as he talked.

"Yes. I can't believe you got me an elephant! I love it. What a wonderful surprise. Thank you."

"You'll get an email every month about Makkoka with an update on his progress and new pictures. You've adopted him for a year. We can extend the adoption if you would like."

"Let's do it. It's a great gift, Tanner. I love the picture too."

"I'm glad you like it. You're hard to buy for. Did you know that?" He took a drink of his Coke.

"No. But you seem to find the perfect gifts."

"Well, I have to work at it."

"Then you need to get busy. Christmas is coming."

"I better hurry."

"Yep. Chop, chop!" She clapped her hands for emphasis. "It's almost time to decorate! Are you getting excited?"

He laughed and ended the call.

"I'll hold the door. Put the boxes labeled 'nativity' in the living room."

After following her initial instructions, the staff brought a plethora of Christmas boxes to the foyer for Angie. They seemed to enjoy working with her. They were her friends, though they probably didn't know it.

"Guys, the new boxes go in the ballroom. The biggest tree will go in the living room again this year." Angie opened a box marked "garland." "The outdoor decorations are stored in the garage storage closets."

"Miss Angie, do you want the Christmas village on the

grand piano again this year?" Maria was personally assigned to set up Joy Ward's favorite pieces.

"Yes, please. Let's keep some of her things the same. I want her memory to live on." Angie took a deep breath and blew it out. "I miss her, Maria."

"I do too. She was so precious."

They worked together until their task was organized, with the appropriate boxes in the dining room, the living room, the ballroom, and the foyer.

"Before we start decorating, would you three men set up the tables in the ballroom? Maria has a diagram of how we want them. Jane, you and Sarah can cover them with our best white tablecloths," Angie said.

They answered in the affirmative and moved to do her bidding.

Angie stuck her head into her grandfather's home office. "Grand-Papa, has the kissing ball been delivered yet? It's almost time to decorate. Maybe I should have brought one home with me."

"It would have slowed us down at customs. Relax. I received notice that it is en route. Scheduled to arrive the first week in December." Ward paused. "Has everything else been delivered?"

"Yes, it's all in the appropriate rooms. With the help of the staff, Tanner and I will get everything done. It'll be spectacular."

"I have no doubt." He hesitated. "Don't feel you must duplicate your grandmother's work, Angelica. Decorate how you want to." He smiled at her and went back to his laptop.

Though Angie heard his words, she still felt pressure to reach the standard set before her. She took a deep breath and hurried to give additional instructions to the staff. As the workers decorated the front porch, she turned to her bodyguard and Grand-Papa's driver. "James, would you and Ellis hang the two large wreaths on the columns at the gate?"

"Yes, we can. Are you going to stay here with the staff?" Ellis asked.

"Don't worry. I won't leave the main house." Anxious to start, she draped a lighted garland down the staircase and added velvet bows and holly, adjusting until everything was perfect. She decorated the dining room table and side tables while Christmas music filled the area. The festive arrangements brought her grandmother to mind. She'd chosen glitzy candelabras, and Angie decided to use them yearly.

"That's beautiful. Nana Joy would be pleased." Ward stopped by the dining table, coffee cup in hand.

"Does it bother you to see her decorations?"

"Not at all. It brings back wonderful memories." He headed toward the kitchen but stopped and pivoted. "Is Tanner going to show up soon?"

"Yes, sir. He'll be here tomorrow." Angie made a big red bow as they talked.

"I need to see both of you for a few minutes tomorrow. Let me know when would be a good time. I'll be working in my home office."

"Sure, Grand-Papa." She reached for another strand of ribbon but paused. "What do you want to talk to us about?"

When she turned around, he wasn't there. He must have returned to the kitchen for those fresh-baked cookies she was smelling. After a few more bows, she decided she would grab some herself.

Tanner smiled as he neared the estate. Even though he lived in the employee section, the place was still home to him. His mother was his only family, and her talents shined at Christmas time. Parking his Hummer near the kitchen door, he heard Christmas music and smelled pies baking. Home.

His mom had a mixer going, drowning out his arrival. He slipped his hand around her and stuck a finger into the icing. She swatted his hand. "Tanner, you're home."

He licked his finger and hugged her. "And hungry."

"You're always hungry, but I love feeding you. Have a seat." She removed the beaters from the mixer and handed Tanner one while she licked the other. "You okay?"

"Yeah. I'm tired but good. I finished my thesis."

"That's wonderful. I'm proud of you." She took the beater from him and dropped both of them in some soapy water in the sink. "I want to hear all about it."

Tanner saw she'd added two photos to her collection on the shelf. "You framed these?" He picked one up.

"You bet. The staff and I laughed and laughed when they came. Kissing a giraffe doesn't happen every day." She smiled. "She pulled one over on you, didn't she?"

"Yep. Again."

Maria laughed. "How about a sandwich?"

"Sure. So, what's Angie been up to?"

"Studying a lot since your Kenya trip, but focused on Christmas decorating now. She's been making some changes."

"She told me she wants to do something special for the employees' children this year." Tanner took a Coke out of the fridge and opened it.

"Does that include you? You're my son." Maria prepared the makings for a sandwich.

"I think I'm a bit old to join the little ones around the Christmas tree." He smiled.

Angie's messy bun bounced as she sorted the limbs of the new Christmas tree into designated piles in the ballroom. Christmas music, a silly reindeer sweater, and bubble gum in her mouth revealed her festive mood. She looked up to see Tanner staring, leaning his handsome body against the doorframe and wearing a grin.

"Don't you just love Christmas?" Angie put two limbs in the correct pile.

"I do, but it looks different on you for some reason." He moved closer and began assembling the trunk of the Christmas tree. "I think you're addicted to Christmas."

She paused in thought. "I guess I am." She reached for another limb. "My folks have always made it special, and as my family has dwindled … I love doing it for others. It keeps me from dwelling on those I miss this time of year."

"Well then, we better get busy. How tall is this tree anyway?"

"Ten feet. That's why I had the ladder brought in for you." She pointed to where it leaned against the wall. "It's got to be perfect."

"Let's create your vision, Ang." He opened the ladder and climbed the rungs.

She handed him the top piece of the white tree and then hurried to the foyer to search through a box.

"Angie, where did you go? I need some help up here in the nosebleed section," Tanner said from his elevated position.

She returned with a beautiful angel in an ice-blue gown with silver wings. "Here, this goes on top." She lifted the piece to him. "There's a plug that has to be connected before we finish the rest of the tree."

When the light came on, she gasped. "Perfect."

He turned toward her. "Me or the angel?"

She swatted his leg with the next two limbs. "I meant the angel, but you're quite fetching, Mr. Zarello. Now get to work."

They worked in tandem as Christmas music filled the room, creating a snow-white tree with white lights and blue-and-silver accents.

Alexander Ward peeked into the ballroom. "I love the tree, Angelica."

"I'm glad you approve, Grand-Papa."

"I do." He paused. "When you two take a break, I want to see you." Ward headed toward the kitchen.

"I'll check with the slave driver and come soon, sir." Tanner closed the ladder and leaned it by the wall.

"Slave driver? You're the one who didn't want to slow down for a break." She placed a silver tree skirt around the base of the new tree. "I'll get us a drink, and we can meet with my grandfather."

"Make mine a Coke with pellet ice." He spoke to her receding figure as she left the room.

Tanner reached Alexander Ward's office before Angie. "Sir, can I ask you something?"

"Sure, what is it?" Ward put his pen down and gave Tanner his attention.

"Did Ellis give you the information on the paparazzi we encountered at the airport?"

"Yes, and I have someone checking into it. I want to find out who his boss is. Thanks for helping Angie when he shoved that microphone in her face."

"You're welcome, sir. But there's something about him. I think he's a stalker. He seems more possessive than a hired photographer would normally be."

"Really?" He paused, making a note on a tablet. "I'll mention this possibility to the officer investigating him." He rubbed his chin. "Let's keep it between us, okay?"

"No problem, sir."

"Make yourself comfortable, Tanner. I think I hear Angie."

"Hey, what's up?" Angie handed Tanner a glass and sat in a leather chair opposite her grandfather's desk.

Tanner took the seat beside her.

"I've received an email from Kenya," Ward said, "and Vice President Saitoti will be in Dallas in January to meet the family of his soon-to-be son-in-law. He asked if they could visit the estate and have a special dinner for the occasion. I've taken the liberty of answering in the affirmative. I want the two of you to plan and host the event."

"When is it, Grand-Papa?"

"January fifth, right before you both go back to school."

Angie put her glass on a coaster and pulled up the calendar on her cell. "That's a Saturday. You up for it, Tanner?" She looked at him.

"Sure. They were kind to us while we were in Kenya. Let's do it."

Angie retrieved a tablet from her grandfather's desk drawer and returned to her chair. "How many people will there be? Do you want a formal dinner or just hors d'oeuvres and drinks?"

"I'd like hors d'oeuvres upon their arrival. Forty people counting us three, and I'd like a formal dinner," Ward said.

"Five, six, or seven courses?"

"Six is good."

"Do we send invitations? Any gifts you'd like to purchase to give the vice president?"

"No invitations, and yes, I would like to provide gifts. I'll get back to you on that."

Angie made notes as Ward answered.

"Sure. Seven o'clock dinner followed by chai and pie served in the ballroom decorated in a winter scene, serenaded by a quintet of strings." She looked up. "Anything else?"

"Sounds like you've got it covered."

Angie stood. "We'll talk with Sarah and Maria. Consider it done."

"Great meeting, sir." Tanner stood. "She'll get it done." He smiled and followed Angie out of the office.

She turned and poked him in the chest. "Don't think you're putting all the work on me." She glared.

"You sounded like a professional in there. What do you need me for?"

"A score of decisions need to be made. We'll tackle the project when we get this place decorated. Don't disappear on me."

He saluted Angie like he would a drill sergeant, then winked. "Yes, ma'am."

"Don't be cute, Tanner." She turned and started for the living room.

"Can't help it. It comes naturally." He laughed out loud.

"I have big snowflakes to hang around the room. All linens and table decorations will be in white, ice blue, and silver. It's a complete change from the décor we've traditionally used, but with Nana Joy gone, I thought Grand-Papa would want something different this year." Angie shared her vision with Tanner.

"Sounds like a great plan." After Tanner finished hiding the extension cords and stood back to admire his work, Angie pushed a stack of boxes into the room. "Here are the decorations for this tree."

"I'll open the boxes while you get us some hot chocolate. Deal?" The sounds of ripping tape pierced the air.

"Deal."

By the end of the evening, the room glowed blue and silver. The tree's sparkling lights reflected off the glossy wood floor.

"It's magical." Angie pivoted, viewing it from all angles. "Thanks, Tanner."

He bowed. "My pleasure."

"Can you help me tomorrow? The staff decorated the front entrance, and I have new lighted trees for the walkway."

"Sounds good. How about after breakfast?"

"Yep. Meet you right here."

After he left, Angie slipped into the dining room and tied large red bows on the chairs to match the table linens, adding a Nana Joy touch to the décor. Angie smiled and then called it a day.

Tanner entered the foyer and found Angie on the ladder, hanging a strand of garland around the front door. "You look cute up there, but I thought the ladder escapades were reserved for me?"

Angie smiled and turned too quickly, causing the ladder to wobble. She grabbed the door frame, trying to find purchase, but failed. "Help!"

Tanner rushed forward and caught her. "Well, good morning to you, Angelica. You look quite fetching today." Face-to-face with Tanner, her breath came quickly. "I'm glad you're breathing this time." He smiled.

"No reason for mouth-to-mouth." She grinned back at him, enjoying their closeness.

He looked up. "What—no mistletoe?"

"Not yet. But I'm not finished." She looked around. "Do you have a hero complex or something?"

"Yes, it's my goal in life to show up before you hurt yourself. What were you doing up there, Ang?"

"I had to start without you. You were late." She held up the garland that had fallen with her.

"Four minutes late. That's no reason to risk your life. Do you think you can stand? We're not getting anything accomplished like this."

"Yep, thanks." She wrapped the garland around his neck. "You're up. Now put me down."

He did as she asked.

Working together, they had the foyer looking like Santa's workshop in no time, with three small trees next to the coat rack and a large sleigh piled high with fake presents.

"I love how Nana Joy matched these decorations to the staircase garland. I want to keep using her designs," Angie said.

Moving to the living room, Tanner recruited a couple of guys to help him with the massive tree while Angie organized the decorations.

Alexander Ward entered, using a cane to walk. "The foyer looks great, guys."

"Step into the ballroom, Grand-Papa. It's amazing," Angie said from the second-story balcony.

"Tanner, here's the tree topper for this one." She reached out to hand it to him. When he took it, he almost lost his balance and grabbed Angie's arm to steady himself. "Don't worry, Tanner. I'll catch you."

"I think I'm a little heavy for a powder puff." He reestablished his footing, released Angie's arm, and put the lighted topper on the tree.

"Well, Macho Man, this powder puff can get this work done. Ellis will help me."

"And miss all this fun? I don't think so." He whistled "All I Want for Christmas is You" along with the music as he climbed down the ladder.

~

The living room at the Ward Estate had hosted scores of important people through the ages. Gold frames decorated the walls with family portraits, matted photos of Angie at different ages were set up by a professional, and an oil rendering of Alexander and Joy Ward was prominently displayed under portrait lighting. Growing up in this environment, Angie no longer paid attention to the Persian rugs, imported French furniture, and chandeliers that created the austere décor. To her, it was just home.

Angie began to open the boxes with the Bethlehem village and nativity scene. She had cleared the coffee table to display them.

"Aren't you getting tired?" Tanner handed her a mug of apple cider. "You've been at this all day—actually, for several days."

"I'm almost done. But, yes. I'm exhausted." She took the mug and made herself comfortable on the soft leather sofa across from the fireplace.

Tanner added some wood to the fire and joined her on the couch. "The place is looking great. Lots of variety. Is that what you were going for?" He took his shoes off and put his feet on the coffee table, crossing his ankles.

"Yep. I have memories connected to each part. I remember my grandmother adding to the Christmas village each year until it filled the top of the piano. I love the village, but my favorite is this Bethlehem scene. My dad bought it for my mom on Catalina Island and had it shipped to our home in Fort Worth." She picked up the cradle holding baby Jesus. "I need to confess—I broke Jesus' head off the first year we displayed the scene. I cried and cried. We couldn't find the head, but my dad called and had another Jesus sent overnight. He saved the day."

"He was your hero. I can see it on your face."

"Yes, he was the best." She paused. "Then ... he was gone. I'll always love this Bethlehem scene with thoughts of my dad ..." She wiped her eyes and continued. "And because it highlights the real reason for the season—the nativity."

"Me too." Tanner took Jesus from her hand and set Him back in the manger.

Missing her parents, Angie sipped her cider, set her cup on the coffee table, and reached for her tablet. Time for a segue. "Can we talk about the VP event? I'll finish the decorating tomorrow."

"Sure, but I don't know how to help. I was impressed listening to you when your grandfather asked us about it. You really know this stuff, don't you?" He placed his empty cup on the table by hers.

"These events have happened all my life, so I do have a bit of experience to fall back on. But before I can proceed, we need to make a few decisions. I'll call the caterer, but we must decide on the menu. What do you think about having soup, salad, two meat options with three vegetables, and a selection of bread?" She sat, poised to take notes.

"Sounds good to me, but they don't eat salads. They like a slaw or cabbage."

"You're right. I'll change the dish to cabbage. What meats would they like?"

"Well, how about baked ostrich and roasted goat?" He laughed.

"I'm not sure my grandfather has ever served those. Give me more suggestions."

"I'd stay away from seafood. What about fried chicken and a great steak? It's very American, and our chickens have more meat on their bones. And if you have the meats prepared by the chef mom used last Easter, it'll be amazing."

She wrote down his suggestions. "What should we serve for dessert? We need three."

"We're known for apple pie. How about that, chocolate cake, and some flan? They had flan at the celebration in Kenya."

"Great ideas. They drink chai, coffee, room-temperature water, and warm Cokes." She made the drink list and yawned.

"You're tired." He put his hand on her arm, squeezed it, and let go.

"Yes. I had a couple tests this week before the break. Late-night studying is catching up with me."

"We can finish this tomorrow. Why don't you sleep in?"

"Sounds like a plan." She closed her pen and set it on the table with the tablet.

Tanner stood, slipped into his shoes, picked up their mugs, and moved toward the kitchen. "Angie, you're doing a great job."

Her eyes filled with tears at his words. "Thanks. That means a lot. I miss her, Tanner."

"I know you do. Your grandmother was amazing." He paused. "Just like you."

Chapter Six

As quiet snow blanketed the ground, a box arrived at the estate on Friday morning after Thanksgiving. Its return address read "Kenya."

"It's the kissing ball." Angie took the box from Maria, who'd accepted the delivery. Rushing to the kitchen, Angie pulled a drawer open, grabbed some scissors, and sliced the tape. She pulled the mistletoe from the box, holding the branch it was attached to. "It's perfect."

"Maria, please mist this and have the guys hang it from the light over the entryway at the front door. It may need extra wire to hold it in place. The men can figure it out. Mistletoe is parasitic—it draws nutrients from the limb it has attached itself to, so we need to keep this branch watered. Remove these plastic vials at the ends of the wood and refill them every few days. It will help keep the plant alive."

"Sure thing, Miss Angie. I'll take care of it." She took the box. "This place looks incredible. Your grandmother would approve."

"I hope you're right. Christmas without her is difficult, but thanks for the compliment. Tanner was a big help."

"He complained about you being a slave driver, but he said it with a smile and hurried back to help you." She turned and started toward the kitchen. "Need anything?"

"No, I'm good. I've got some reports due next week, so I'm going to be working this weekend." She turned toward her end of the estate, then pivoted. "On second thought, I think I'll work in here by the tree. Could you have Ellis start a fire for me and leave a wood supply?"

"I'll get James to do it for you. Today is Ellis's wedding anniversary, and he's taking his wife out. He said he's wearing his blue suede shoes and plans to be a hunka, hunka burning love." Maria laughed as she texted the firewood request.

Angie grinned. "I'd like to see that." Her phone chimed. She looked at the screen and smiled. Tanner.

"Hi, Tanner."

"Hello. You busy?"

"I was just talking to your mother. So ... I'm still a slave driver." She smiled to herself.

"Yep. I had to get back to the university to rest."

"Oh, you poor thing."

"That doesn't sound very sincere, Miss Ward."

"Since hard work is good for you, I think I'm doing you a great service by allowing you to do manual labor from time to time."

"I appreciate you looking out for me, Ang. And it looks great. I hope your grandfather was pleased."

"He was. He asked if you and I would host the Christmas Bash he throws for his employees and their families. I think it's hard for him to do it without my grandmother at his side. You game?"

"Sure. What do we have to do?"

"Welcome guests, take their coats, make announcements, hand out presents—stuff like that."

"Doesn't sound hard. Tell him we'll do it, and text me the date."

"Okay. Have you been busy?"

"I have a heavy workload between now and Christmas break."

"Yeah, me too."

"Dylan just arrived with pizza. We're studying most of the weekend. Dylan's fiancé is having a bridesmaids thing for the next few days. Have a good weekend, Ang.

"Don't work too hard."

"Now you tell me!"

Freezing rain pelted his windshield as Tanner left the university. The bite in the air on this mid-December morning caused his truck's heater to labor, but salt on the roads kept him safe and on schedule. With a promise of a sunny afternoon in the forecast, tonight's event wouldn't be canceled.

A catering truck, two flower delivery vans, and an unidentified truck were parked at the front of the Ward Estate when Tanner pulled in. After parking his Hummer, he made his way through the vehicles. Glancing in the window of the unmarked Ford, he saw an expensive camera in the passenger seat, partially covered by a jacket. *Not very secure.* The passenger-side door was locked, but the driver's side wasn't. *Why would a worker have an expensive camera in his truck? This place is secure, but that's taking a big chance.* He hurried into the estate to help Angie with last-minute details.

Entering the estate was like stepping into a winter wonderland. The elaborate decorations, the lights, and the smells would make even Scrooge nostalgic. Angie's voice overrode the noise of the work in progress. Dressed in exercise attire, tennis shoes, and sporting a ponytail, she gave orders to the staff like a woman on a mission.

"We're not using my grandmother's Christmas china this year. Let's use the white china with the silver chargers on white linens. Sarah, the silver table runners will add a perfect touch. They're in the linen room. Would you get those, please?"

"Sure. You want to use the silver-rimmed stemware?" Sarah asked.

"Yes. Maria can show you where they're stored."

Tanner loved seeing Angie in action. She may be filthy rich, but she didn't shy away from hard work, and she had the staff in the palm of her hand.

She scanned her clipboard and then faced the audio team. "When you guys complete your soundcheck, I want to see the Christmas playlist. "Grandma Got Run Over by a Reindeer" won't work this year. And I want to discuss the evening's agenda."

Looking closer, Tanner noticed one of the audio team members looked familiar. He wore a ball cap backward over his shaggy brown hair and held his cell phone against his chest as if hoping no one would notice. An employee had no reason to be on his phone. Tanner eased toward the gathering unnoticed. Once close to the culprit, he realized who he was and what he was doing. *Not again.*

"Paparazzi!" In one swift move, Tanner grabbed the cell phone. "Angie, call security!" The guy swung at Tanner, nicking his chin with the ring on his right hand. Tanner retaliated with a hit of his own and knocked him to the floor. With his knee on the photographer's back, he held his phone out of reach and scanned the photos on it. "Angie, is your grandfather here?"

"No, he's still at his downtown office. I'll call him." She'd backed away to join the kitchen staff by the wall.

Ellis rushed in with his gun drawn. Tanner grabbed the guy's arm and twisted it behind him to keep him from bolting.

"It's not against the law to take pictures! Let me go. I was hired on this crew." He spit saliva with his words.

"I warned you to stay away from her. We're pressing charges this time." Tanner walked him across the large room.

"But she's mine! I've worked hard to get this assignment. Angie, your story needs to be in the tabloids, and I need the money. Don't you understand?" He stared at Angie with pleading eyes. "I'm trying to help you. People eat this up! The Ward name means prestige, power, and dollar signs. With my name on the byline, I can make a killing." He struggled to free himself.

"You almost killed her for your story. So shut it!" Tanner shoved him out of the ballroom toward Ellis, who had him in his sites. Sirens screamed in the distance as they forced him out the front door to wait for the authorities, allowing Angie and her team to catch their breath and stay on point—if they could.

Angie looked around the room. "Everybody okay?"

They nodded their heads.

"Are you, Miss Angie?" Sarah moved closer to her. "Can I get you a bottle of water or something?"

"Water would be great, Sarah."

She looked at the staff. "Hey guys, let's take a ten-minute break before we start working again."

They moved, talking softly among themselves. Angie stood still and rubbed her hands up and down her arms. The paparazzi had gotten closer this time—inside the estate, a few feet from her. *Too close for comfort.*

"Drink, Miss Angie." Sarah gave her a cold bottle of water and brought a chair close. "Sit for a minute. Get your bearings."

Sarah pulled another chair over and sat with her. "We trust the Lord to take care of us, Miss Angie. The enemy got close, but He sent Tanner at the right moment. This guy has met his match with Zarello, Ellis, and your grandfather. They'll make mincemeat out of him."

Angie smiled. "I'd like to see that, but right now, we have a job to do." She took a deep breath, a long drink of cold water, and stood. "Okay, group. Let's get busy and finish ahead of schedule."

As the tenseness of the paparazzi episode dissipated, the staff relaxed and helped Angie create a Christmas wonderland for the loyal employees of Ward Enterprises. By six o'clock, the ballroom was ready, the food smelled wonderful, and Christmas music wafted through the estate. Angie breathed a sigh of relief.

Tanner entered the main foyer and whistled. "You look stunning, Ang."

Wearing a burgundy velvet cocktail dress with Swarovski-crystal trim and matching stilettos, she pivoted like a model at the end of a runway, giving him the full effect of her attire.

"Thank you, kind sir. You don't look so bad yourself, Zarello. Is that a tux?"

"Yep—gotta look the part." He smiled.

"Well, you do look amazing. Thanks for saving the day this afternoon. I'm glad you showed up when you did. I never expected him to be so brazen as to infiltrate our event for a photo—or a story. I assume you and Ellis took care of him."

"Yeah. If he owns a drone, we may have found our culprit. If I'm right, he'll face charges."

"And he was right here in the estate—standing in front of me. That scares me, Tanner." She rubbed her arms with trembling hands.

He took her hands in his. "Don't dwell on it. We can talk it through later. You have to be a welcoming hostess in just a few minutes. It's your superpower. You stuff your personal issues down deep to deal with later and perform, perfectly finishing the task at hand. So, are you ready?"

"I am. Want to see the ballroom? It sparkles like Elsa's ice castle."

"Should I sing 'Let It Go'?"

The doorbell sounded with "Deck the Halls."

"Let's pass on the singing, but you can answer the door." She smiled.

"But I thought you loved my singing." He moved toward the front door.

"I like it when you sing far, far away." Angie laughed.

In a matter of minutes, the place was filling with guests. Alexander Ward seemed to enjoy mingling among the crowd. Tanner and Angie kept things moving, making sure everyone was happy. The buffet proved successful, as well as the dessert bar and chocolate fountains.

Tanner filled a plate and found Angie looking bored by Mason Malone's self-serving diatribe. He stood close and listened.

"Angelica, think about it. Working together, we can take Ward Enterprises to another level. With you on my arm, we would be a handsome couple, and our involvement in social circles would benefit the company financially."

Tanner rolled his eyes. It took restraint to keep from slugging the guy.

"I don't see how it would help Ward Enterprises," Angie responded. "The company is making amazing strides at this time without added personal publicity. I'd rather not be in the limelight. The face of the company is Alexander Ward. Speaking of my grandfather, have you mentioned your ideas to him?" Angie eased away from the pushy guy.

Interrupting their conversation, Tanner said, "Mason, grab yourself a plate, man. The kids are scarfing it down fast."

"I guess I should. But I wanted your thoughts first. I'll talk to you before I leave, Angelica." Mason touched her arm. "Think about my suggestion." He ignored Tanner, turned, and perused the food tables.

Tanner handed Angie a plate. "You looked like you needed rescuing, and you haven't eaten a thing. You need to eat. It's going to be a long night."

Angie accepted the display of delicacies. "You've chosen my favorites, and I'm famished. I didn't eat lunch."

"The evening is a success. Just listen. Laughter, forks hitting china, children's giggles, and Christmas music. The sounds memories are made of."

"I'm glad. It's good for Ward Enterprises employees and the staff at the estate to be blessed at Christmas. Get some dessert before we start handing out gifts."

"Okay. Save me a place at your table. I'll be right there."

Tanner reached over the heads of children surrounding the fountains to scoop up some chocolate. After grabbing a handful of strawberries and a handful of pretzels, he eased to the other end of the table to get three petit fours for Angie. Greeting people along the way, he took a seat by Angie. "I managed to snag three of these little cakes before they disappeared."

"My favorites." She reached for a petit four.

"I remember when you snuck into the kitchen and ate so

many of these you got sick." He swirled a strawberry in his chocolate and took a bite.

"You remember that?" She bit into the confection-covered cake with a red poinsettia on top.

"Of course. It took you two years to try them again." He dipped a pretzel in his chocolate."Here comes your grandfather."

"Great party, you two. I appreciate your hard work." Alexander Ward put his hand on Tanner's shoulder. "Who wants to hand these out?" Ward laid a stack of vellum envelopes on their table.

Angie leaned forward. "Grand-Papa, you usually do that. You don't want to continue the tradition?"

"No. You've changed things up this year and it worked. Let's change this part too." He turned to speak to Mason Malone, who probably wanted to be included in the envelope distribution.

"You do it, Angie. You're his granddaughter." Tanner handed them to her.

"How about we do it together?" They stood, divided the envelopes, and called the gathering to order. Like game show hosts, they proceeded with the presentation of bonuses by calling them forward one by one.

As they presented the last bonus check, Ward stepped to the microphone. "As a bonus for those employed at Ward Enterprises, we're not working between Christmas and New Year's. Enjoy your time off, with pay, of course. We will resume our regular schedule on January second. Those employed here at the estate will have an abbreviated schedule. Maria has that information. Merry Christmas to each of you."

Applauds erupted as Ward moved to the chair by the Christmas tree.

"Now, could all the children sit on the floor around the

white Christmas tree?" Angie spoke into the mic. "We have something special for you."

Within minutes, the giggling group was seated, anticipating the final moments of the party. Ward seemed to enjoy their laughter. Angie and Tanner took ornaments off the tree and handed them to Ward. He called each name and hugged each child when he presented their gift. Their squeals filled the ballroom as they opened their presents, finding a hundred-dollar bill to buy a toy of their choice and a miniature gift card for a free ice cream every week of the new year.

As the evening began to wind down, Angie and Tanner helped retrieve coats for their departing guests.

"Grand-Papa is still smiling. I think he enjoyed blessing the children," Angie said, watching him from the foyer.

"He did. Great idea, Angie."

"I'm glad. I hope they felt valued. They're special to us. It was good for Grand-Papa to have something to smile about— to forget about his loss for a few moments."

Mason Malone stepped forward and wrapped Angie in a hug, holding her too close for too long. She turned her head so he wouldn't consider kissing her.

"Angelica, I put a gift for you under the tree in the living room."

"Thank you, Mason. That's not necessary." Angie stepped out of his embrace.

He touched her cheek. "Oh, I disagree. It's a special gift for a special lady."

"Malone, here's your trench coat." Tanner extended it, forcing Mason to step back to retrieve it. "Drive carefully, Mason. Have a good night." Before he had time to close his coat, Tanner opened the door for him.

Mason leaned in and kissed Angie on the cheek. "I hope to see you soon, Angelica. Merry Christmas." He leaned forward and kissed her forehead. "Consider what we talked about. Together, you and I could take Ward Enterprises to a new level. Once we join forces, there's no limit to what we can accomplish. We can share a great future."

Tanner interrupted. "Angie, some of the little girls want to say goodnight." When Angie turned toward the girls, Tanner shut the door on Mason Malone.

Angie smiled at Tanner's dismissal of Mason as she knelt to hug three girls and help with their coats before bidding them and their parents good night.

Tanner retrieved his mother's coat when she entered the foyer.

"This was beautiful. Splendid, in fact. Great job, you two." Maria allowed Tanner to help her with her coat.

"Thanks, Maria," Angie said.

"Goodnight, Mom." He kissed her cheek. "I'm glad you came through the front door instead of the kitchen tonight."

"I'm honored to do it once a year." She patted Tanner's arm.

He opened the door and asked James to walk her home before closing it, shutting out the cold air.

"How many more are still here?" Angie slipped one shoe off and rubbed the arch of her foot. "I can't wait to shed these stilettos."

Tanner left to look into the ballroom and returned. "Fifteen to twenty guests are waiting to speak to your grandfather. Won't be long now."

Angie held his arm, steadying herself while she put her shoe back on. "Tanner, grab the fur coat at the end of the row. The chairman of the board and his wife are coming this way."

Within fifteen minutes, all the guests had departed. Angie shut the door for the final time and shivered.

With the ballroom empty, Ward walked toward Angie,

using his cane. "Excellent job, you two. The changes you added made the night spectacular. Everyone had a wonderful time." Alexander Ward started upstairs.

"See you tomorrow, Grand-Papa. Get some rest. You look tired."

"Good night, sir." Tanner watched Ward's slow departure.

"Night."

"He's exhausted," Angie said.

"It has been a long day."

"Yeah, but what a night." She smiled.

"You made it a merry Christmas for so many."

"I hope so." Angie removed her shoes.

"I have a question, Ang. What's that?" He pointed up at the ball of greenery above the door. "That wasn't here when we decorated."

"That, my friend, is a kissing ball." She smiled. "I ordered it from Kenya. Mistletoe grows in balls in the trees around Mt. Kenya. The vice president exports roses to Europe each week. I had my grandfather ask him to send this to me. And he did!"

"That sounds like a lot of trouble for a plant."

"But it's not just any plant—it's a kissing ball." She glanced up at the mistletoe and moved closer. "It offers an opportunity to those standing under it to express their heart to someone special during the Christmas season." Angie dropped her shoes, rose on her tip-toes, grabbed the lapels on his jacket, and kissed him.

"That's why I went to all that trouble." She could feel his breath on her face as their gazes locked.

Tanner took her hands and placed them around his neck,

then slipped his arms around her. He kissed her softly at first, then tightened his embrace and deepened the kiss.

Angie melted into him. Being in his arms felt amazing. It was a perfect moment. The perfect kiss, and so worth the wait. She didn't want it to end.

Tanner gently brushed a stray hair across her forehead when they eased apart. "Thanks for going to so much trouble, Ang." He winked, smiled, kissed her forehead, and left her standing under the kissing ball with stars in her eyes.

She couldn't move. Didn't want to. The kissing ball was magic. It worked! She wanted to bask in the lingering softness of his touch. Tanner had kissed her. Not just a peck on the cheek, but a real kiss. One she would never forget.

"Miss Angie, sorry to bother you. I was doing a final check of the doors and wanted to lock this one for the night." Ellis stood, waiting for her to move.

She stepped away from the door. "Sure. You have a job to do. I just let out our last guest." She picked up her shoes and headed to her end of the estate. "Good night, Ellis."

"Night, Miss Angie."

Questions whirled in her mind as she left the foyer. How would their kiss change their relationship? Should she mention it again or act like it never happened? Did it mean as much to Tanner as it did to her?

On her way to her end of the estate, she replayed the scene, memorizing every detail. It was a perfect Christmas moment under the mistletoe. *But now, how do I top that?*

That was a mistake.

Once behind the wheel of his Hummer, Tanner replayed their moment under the mistletoe. He didn't expect her kiss, but when it offered itself, he'd taken advantage of the opportunity.

Angie's eyes had sparkled when she initiated the kiss. She'd put a lot of thought and planning into creating the moment they'd shared. Ordering a kissing ball from Kenya and having it shipped ten thousand miles to Dallas took effort. She did it because she wanted to kiss him. It changed everything, but how would it change their friendship? *And where do we go from here?*

Once he reached his meager loft apartment, Tanner slipped on some jogging pants and lay across his bed. He had to be the logical one—the one to set the pace. He should consider several things. Being aware of her status (she was worth millions, and he was the maid's son) put them miles apart on a social level. Unreachable.

The moment was amazing—life-altering—but he knew which end of the estate he came from. Friendship was all he could ever have with Angelica Ward. He'd play it cool. He decided to not make a big deal of their mistletoe moment and let it fade as the season passed. He saw no other choice.

Before her feet hit the floor, Angie grabbed her phone. "Morning, Tanner."

"You're up early. I thought you'd sleep in."

"I had something on my mind."

"And what was that?"

"Are we going to talk about the elephant in the room? Sarah would call it the pachyderm in the parlor."

"Nope."

"Nope?"

Silence.

"Well, I guess that's that. We'll play it by ear. Now I'm nervous." Angie paused. "Okay, see you later." She hung up, fell back against her pillows, and covered her head.

Chapter Seven

Christmas music filled the air and a fire blazed in the fireplace as Angie munched on Christmas cookies while reclining on the living room sofa with a Christmas novel. The pitter-patter of rain against the windows added to her nostalgic afternoon.

"Comfortable, my dear?" Her grandfather stole a cookie off her plate.

She smiled. "Yes. Nana and I enjoyed doing this after a day of Christmas shopping. I miss her, but I wanted to keep up our tradition. My feet are tired from walking the mall this morning looking for gifts. Ellis is probably exhausted from following me from store to store, but he's handy at carrying packages." She offered him the plate, and he took a reindeer-shaped cookie. "I hope talking about Nana doesn't make you sad."

"Everything adds to my grief this first Christmas. The music, the decorations, the gifts, and the date on the calendar all cause a void nothing can fill. But don't concern yourself. While remembering the ones we've lost, I don't want to miss special time with you, Angelica."

"Sounds like a plan."

"I'm glad you agree, because I've spent a lot of money to put a smile on your face on Christmas morning." He put another big log on the fire. "Enjoy your book."

"Thanks, Grand-Papa. Can I ask you a question?"

"Sure, what is it?" He slapped his hands together, dusting dirt and bark off them.

"I have a faint memory of my dad kissing Mom on her forehead. Did he do that often?" She watched him rub his goatee.

"Yeah, he did it from time to time. He said it was because he cherished her like a rare gem of great worth. He would say, 'You're priceless.' Your mother smiled every time."

"They really loved each other, didn't they?"

"Yes, they did."

"Thanks, Grand-Papa. Hope you rest well."

"You too. Why don't you get yourself some hot chocolate?" He grabbed another Christmas cookie and headed toward his bedroom.

"Good idea." She went to the kitchen as Maria entered from her apartment.

"Maria, I thought you were gone for the day." Angie retrieved a mug from the cabinet, placed it in the Keurig, and started her hot chocolate. "It's good to see you in jeans and a T-shirt, and look at those comfy socks!"

"Oh, I've been gone for some time—thus the jeans. I do tire of wearing black slacks, white tops, and aprons. But I don't mind it. It's proper."

"What are you doing tonight?" Angie checked the Keurig's progress.

"Tanner's been helping me with my Christmas tree. I shouldn't have bought such a large one, but I like it." She closed a plastic container of Christmas cookies. "I promised Tanner some of my cookies if he would put it up for me."

"So you're paying the help?"

"I am. He's a good son. You did such a wonderful job at the party last night. Everyone had a great time." She wiped crumbs off the kitchen counter. "Seeing your grandfather smile was refreshing."

"I couldn't have done it without Tanner's help." Grabbing a spoon, Angie stirred her steamy beverage.

"He is pretty amazing." Maria turned to leave.

"I agree with you there." Angie smiled at the memory they made under the kissing ball.

Tanner was adjusting the top of the tree when his mom came in with some cookies. "Does it look straight to you?" He held his hand out for a cookie.

She gave him two cookies, eyed the Douglas fir, and gave him a thumbs-up. "It's perfect. I like the shape."

"Do you have a topper? I could put it on for you."

She opened a box and pulled out a new topper. "I want this lighted star on there this year. Can you plug it in for me?"

"Sure." He did as she requested and joined her at the table for some cookies. "These are good, Mom." He took another bite. "Want me to help you put the ornaments on?"

"No, but thanks. You've done enough. I can finish it."

He stood. "You got some more of those cookies?"

"I have a container ready. When I went to the estate kitchen for your cookies, Angie was making herself some hot chocolate."

"She was?" He put his coat on and reached for his keys.

"Yeah, and she smiled when I mentioned you." Maria stood, retrieved a mug, and poured herself a cup of coffee. "You have feelings for her, don't you? I don't want you to get your heart broken."

With his hand on the front door, he turned back. "I'm being careful. I know I'm from the wrong side of the estate, but we're best friends. Have been since we were kids."

"I know that, but I saw your hackles go up last night when Mason Malone made his play. I'm just concerned." She joined him at the front door.

"Don't worry, Mom. It'll be okay. I promise." He kissed her cheek, went to his truck, and left for his loft apartment. *I can't get anything past her.* She could read a room faster than anyone he knew. Working at the estate for so many years, she'd become close with the Wards. She had keen insight concerning their status and their importance to society. And she was right to be concerned. Could a maid's son ever be worthy of the stunning beauty of Ward Enterprises?

When Angie met an array of eligible suitors trying to win her heart, would she remember her childhood hero—the young man who kissed her under the kissing ball? *Probably not.*

With two days left until Christmas, Angie wrapped gifts and placed them under the appropriate trees. Her and Grand-Papa's gifts went under the large tree in the living room, where they would exchange gifts on Christmas morning by a roaring fire.

She put Tanner's gifts under the tree they'd decorated in the foyer. Ever since they were in their early teens, they'd met in the estate's foyer on the winding staircase each year around noon, before their separate Christmas dinners. When she set the first gift under the tree, she saw three presents with her name on them and shook each one.

Her phone rang. Tanner.

"Hey, Ang. You busy?"

"Not really. Just wrapping presents. What's up?"

"I'm with Mom. I bought her a new television for Christmas, and I'm installing it. Could we discuss the preparations for the vice president's event while I'm here?"

"Sure. I plan to bring some gifts to the big tree. Grab us some Cokes in the kitchen and meet me in the living room in ten."

"Sounds good."

Tanner came in with a tray of assorted Christmas candies and cookies along with their cold Cokes. "Mom sent refreshments."

"She's been busy. I'm glad she's in charge. Our food is amazing, and things run smoothly because of her." Angie grabbed a piece of peanut brittle and stuck it in her mouth.

"She loves working here." He put the tray on the coffee table and sat a few feet away. "You have your tablet?"

"Yep." Angie reached for her notebook. "I've hired the caterer, and they have our menu. I called a florist and ordered arrangements for the ballroom. Here's a sketch of how I thought we could arrange the room. Look at this and let me know what you think." She handed him the notebook.

She could smell Tanner's woodsy cologne as she leaned closer. "If we put the vice president, his wife, my grandfather, the groom's parents, and the engaged couple here at a head table, there would be seats for two more guests, which the VP could choose."

Tanner touched her hand, sending warmth up her arm. "The diagram looks good. It gives access to the dessert tables and drink station. The staff will serve the meal under silver domes, right?"

"Yes, Grand-Papa loves that. But considering it's a semi-formal affair, the dessert and drink areas are appropriate." She took a sip of her Coke.

"What are we doing for entertainment? Live music or recorded? You had people who took care of this for the Christmas party. Want to use them again?" He released the notebook and reached for his Dr. Pepper.

"I have an idea. What do you think about looking around for some Kenyan musicians to provide the entertainment?"

He clinked the ice in his glass. "I love that idea, Angie. You think you can find some? They have to be exceptional to meet Alexander Ward's expectations."

"It is a tall order, but I've heard of an ensemble that's supposed to be good." She made a note on her tablet.

"If you have time for that. You're here on site." He sampled a couple of candied pecans from their snack tray.

She drew a checkmark on an item on her list. "I've talked with my grandfather, and we've shopped online for the gifts he wants to present. Most of them have arrived, so that's covered. What about the order of events?"

"I could come up with some suggestions and you could run them by your grandfather. Maybe we can have two different plans and let him choose."

"Perfect. Are we forgetting anything?" She reached for another piece of peanut brittle.

"I think you've got it covered. It'll be a wonderful evening, and I think the vice president will be pleased."

Angie closed her notebook. "You got your mom a TV?"

"Yes. Hers was old, and a small line was forming across the screen. I knew it wouldn't last long. I have more gifts under the tree, but I gave her the television early so she can watch her Hallmark Christmas movies." He stood and picked up the tray.

"That was thoughtful. We ladies love Hallmark."

He placed Angie's empty glass on the tray and took three steps backward toward the kitchen. "You love your Christmas movies, lighted trees, roaring fires, Christmas novels, music, and cookies. Gifts must be opened at specific times by specific Christmas trees." He took a few more steps. "And there must be mistletoe!" He winked, turned, and left her with a blush creeping up her neck.

She let out a breath she didn't realize she was holding.

When Christmas morning dawned, a gentle snow fell, adding ambience to the setting. Angie readied herself for a casual breakfast. Opening gifts with Grand-Papa was bittersweet without Nana Joy, but they pressed through. Grand-Papa insisted she open her gifts first. Angie loved the new lens for her Nikon camera. His traditional gift, a piece of jewelry, was a tanzanite tennis bracelet that sparkled under the tree lights. The fluffy robe and comfy slippers were a surprise. A generous gift card peeked out of the pocket of the robe. Though they were probably selected and wrapped by Sarah, the gifts were very thoughtful.

"Grand-Papa, I love my gifts. Open yours." She handed him a stack of gifts.

He tore them open one by one, revealing a new bathrobe and house shoes, a Mont Blanc pen set, a leather-bound journal, and a blanket with pictures of Joy that brought tears to his eyes. "This is so special, Angelica. Perfect, in fact." He wiped his eyes.

"Grand-Papa, would you go for a drive with me? I love

driving in the snow before the roads get icy." She held her key fob and dangled the key.

He pivoted. "I'll meet you in the garage in twenty minutes." Smiling, he continued toward his bedroom, humming, *"Chestnuts roasting on an open fire ... Jack Frost nipping at your nose ..."* as he walked from the room with his blanket draped over his arm. Angie knew she'd always cherish these moments with her grandfather.

~

Angie had her new Lexus warmed up and ready to roll by the time Grand-Papa walked out the front door of the estate. He smiled and climbed into the front seat as James held the door. "You look good in this vehicle, my dear."

"I love it! Feel this white leather. It's so soft. The color of the exterior matches my new bracelet—tanzanite blue. Perfect!" She turned the knob, putting it in gear. "Ready, Grand-Papa?"

"Yes, let's go." He clicked his seat belt in place and relaxed in the heated seat. "You've hibernated at the estate since your semester ended. It's good to see you out enjoying this crisp Christmas morning air."

"When I hibernate, as you call it, there's less chance of another paparazzi encounter."

"Those incidents have affected you, haven't they? I've noticed you're jumpy at sudden noises and quick to defend or explain yourself." Ward sounded worried.

"Yes, I have nightmares some nights, leaving me tired and anxious the next day. But time will help me get past it."

James waved as they reached the front gates, and Angie put her window down.

"Don't fret, James. You still have a job." She raised her

window, cutting off the sound of his laughter. "We have a great staff, don't we?"

"Yes, we do. They're not without faults, but they have wonderful hearts." He watched her profile.

"I'm not sure about Mason's heart. The jury is still out on that one." Angie took the ramp to enter the interstate and brought her Lexus up to speed.

"But he's so good at what he does. He's the first to arrive and the last to leave the office. His work ethic is stellar, Angelica."

"Is he brownnosing his way up the ladder, vying for position?" She changed lanes and took the exit.

"You're pretty hard on Mason. He works diligently for the company. If he is vying for position, I don't see it."

"They say you can't see the forest for the trees. Time will tell. Maybe I'm being too quick to judge, but I think Mason Malone has ulterior motives."

"Maybe you're uncomfortable because he has feelings for you. He'll make his move when you take your position at Ward Enterprises."

"Since he attends functions you and I must attend, Mason always assumes he's my date. I'd rather be considered your plus-one. His arrogance gets on my last nerve."

Letting the subject drop, she took a right turn. Driving through a park, she asked. "Do you miss driving, Grand-Papa?"

"No. I love being chauffeured. It gives me time to prepare for the next meeting, the next big decision. Staying ahead of the game takes focus and instinct."

"I understand that, but what do you do to take your mind off work?" She turned them back toward home. She needed to change clothes before Tanner showed up.

Ward laughed. "About Mason, your impression of him may

change once you see him in action. Didn't he give you a Christmas present?"

"Oh, I forgot. It's still under the tree." She stopped at a light. "This SUV drives like a dream. Thank you again. I appreciate all the ways you've blessed me."

"You're welcome, Angelica. I love putting a smile on your face." He rubbed his hand on the soft leather. "It is a beautiful vehicle. It has some of the highest safety ratings of SUVs this size."

"I want to study the manual. I need to check out all the 'bells and whistles.'" She smiled as she stopped in front of the front door.

He opened the glove compartment and handed her the manual. "I think the whistles are listed in here. Happy reading." He climbed out. "Thanks for the ride."

"Anytime." She watched him enter the estate. He limped with each step. "You're welcome, Grand-Papa," she said aloud, even though he was gone.

After their drive, she dressed in a red cashmere sweater and green leggings and then waited for Tanner. Before leaving her bedroom, she decided it was a perfect day to wear her mother's pearl inlaid locket. She never stopped missing her and her dad.

Waiting by the crackling fire, she read the happily-ever-after ending of her Christmas novel, which put her in a great mood. Hearing the front door, she met Tanner for their annual gift exchange.

"Ho, Ho, Ho. Merry Christmas." He shut the door and took a seat on the stairs.

"Merry Christmas to you too." She retrieved their gifts from under the foyer tree and handed him one. "Here's a gift for you.".

He tore it open as she brought the rest of their gifts to the stairs.

"I love this, Ang. It'll fit my phone perfectly. So you noticed my case was shot?"

"Yes, and this one charges the phone automatically." After presenting him with a larger gift, she waited.

He unwrapped the present and smiled. "This is amazing." He pulled out a leather satchel with his initials engraved on the flap. "Awesome." He hugged her, then pulled back. "I love this leather, Ang. I'll enjoy using it. Now open one of your gifts."

She chose a small one and tore off the wrapping paper. "It's beautiful, Tanner. Put it on me?" She lifted her black hair and turned around. The necklace had an Africa-shaped pendant with a tanzanite stone mounted where Kenya sat on the map. She rubbed her hand over it, feeling the stone. "I love it. You bought this in Kenya, didn't you?"

"Yep. I thought you'd like it." He smiled.

"I really do. Kenya holds a special place in my heart."

"I've seen you wear that locket before. It looks antique. Was it your grandmother's?"

"No, it was my mother's. The story is pretty incredible, but that's for another day." She picked up a gift, put it in his lap, and smiled.

"This feels like a book." He tore it open and grinned. "This isn't supposed to be released until April. How did you get a copy?"

"I have my ways."

"This is great, Ang. Thank you." Tanner gave her another gift just as the song "All I Want for Christmas Is You" began to play. *Did she have that song cued to play for when I'm at the estate?* "See if you like this one." He waited.

She squealed when she saw four black-currant sodas in the box, her favorite drink from Kenya. "If I'd known how good these were sooner, I would have been drinking them the whole time we were there. Did you sneak these home in your luggage?"

"I did."

"I'll have one today to celebrate Christmas." She set them aside.

"Oh no. Are we adding something to our list of traditions?" He shook his head.

"What a good idea!" She tore open a Yeti cup with her name on it. Inside, she found a gold Starbucks gift card that held a large amount. She hugged him. "Thank you."

When they finished their pile of presents, Tanner pulled a small silver drawstring bag from his pocket and presented it to Angie.

She opened the bag and pulled out a toe ring with a small diamond on it. "I love it. It's perfect."

"I asked the lady at the jewelry store, 'What do you get someone who has absolutely everything?' She suggested this."

"Thank you. Smart lady. I don't have one of these." She pulled off her fuzzy socks and put the toe ring on. "Look, Tanner. It's perfect." She held her foot out so he could see her toes.

He smirked. "I'm glad you like it."

"You outdid yourself this year, Tanner Zarello." She kissed his cheek, enjoying their nearness. "Oh, I forgot to tell you." She pulled back. "I received an email, and Mukkoko is doing great—getting into mischief and making new friends."

"Did they send you a picture?"

"Yes, it's on my phone in my room. I'll show it to you later."

Getting to his feet, Tanner collected his gifts and put them in his new satchel. "I love my presents. You put a lot of thought and work into your gift selections, Ang, and it shows. Thanks." He took her hand and helped her stand so that they were face-to-face. "I hope this Christmas season has met all your expectations."

"It has, thanks to you."

The staff began setting food on the dining room table and preparing Christmas dinner for Angie and her grandfather. Their voices carried into the foyer, interrupting their moment. Tanner leaned forward and kissed her forehead. His breath warmed her face.

She met his dark-brown eyes. "Merry Christmas, Tanner." She didn't want their time together to end.

"My gifts are amazing." He put the strap of his satchel on his shoulder. "And so are you." He squeezed her hand, stared at her for a moment, reached out, and pulled her in for a hug.

Memorizing the moment, she wrapped her arms around him and enjoyed his embrace. When he stepped back, she smiled.

"Merry Christmas, Ang." He turned and left.

Tears filled Angie's eyes as Grand-Papa said his traditional Christmas prayer. She was the only one listening—except for the Lord, to whom he was praying. Their loss was magnified by the empty seat at the table beside her grandfather. He had chosen to wear his Christmas bowtie and red plaid sweater-vest over a white button-down dress shirt, the outfit Nana Joy made him wear last year.

"Amen." Angie squeezed his hand. "Merry Christmas, Grand-Papa. Thank you again for my presents. I'm so blessed."

"You're welcome. I love watching you on your birthday and

at Christmas. Your facial expressions when you see my gifts bring me so much joy. You light up."

She began to fill his plate—something Nana Joy had always done for him at Christmas. His eyes filled.

"Hiring Maria was your best decision yet, Grand-Papa. This food is amazing."

He wiped his mouth. "She's the best chef we've had here at the estate." He took a drink of water. "I assume you've seen Tanner today." Ward cut his turkey and dipped it in gravy.

"Yes. We exchanged our gifts earlier. Look at the necklace he gave me." She held the pendant out for him to see. "I love that the tanzanite sits where Kenya is located." She leaned forward so he could see it.

"He made a great choice. It's quite lovely." He reached for the breadbasket. "Will you see Tanner again today?"

She offered him some butter. "I don't think so. He's spending the day with his mom, and some of their family members are in town. You need to talk to him?"

"Yes, I do. But don't bother him on Christmas. Ask him to call me tomorrow?"

"Sure, I'll text him tonight and give him your message."

They filled their time with small talk, and their pleasant day passed without any more tears. Angie was thankful—for her grandfather and for a lifetime of wonderful memories. The Lord had been faithful through every trial, every dark day.

Her friendship with Tanner was the icing on the cake—the whipped cream on the pumpkin pie. Their moment under the kissing ball stood out as the highlight of the season. Pure magic.

～

After a long bath, Angie reclined in her adjustable bed and requested the Hallmark Channel from her remote control. Credits scrolling across the screen let her know she had a few minutes before her movie of choice would begin. She reached for her cell phone when it rang.

"Hi, Tanner. Did you have a Merry Christmas?"

"Yes, I did. But I ate too much. Now I'm watching football in a food coma. What's up?"

"My grandfather wants to talk to you. He'd like you to call him in the morning."

"Sure. I'll call him, or I can stop by before I leave. Did you try out the new lens he got you for Christmas?"

"Yeah. I can stand at my back window and get a close-up of the ducks near the pier. The lens is amazing."

"Enjoy it. Your photography is pretty amazing."

"When did you see any of my pictures?"

"After I found your camera on the pier. I looked through the pics stored in your Nikon. I was looking for photos of the paparazzi or the drone that hit you. You're a great photographer, Ang."

"Thanks, I appreciate that."

"See you tomorrow."

Angie pushed end on her cell, hugged the phone to her heart, and sighed.

Refusing to work on Christmas day, he didn't tell his boss he wasn't standing in freezing temps to watch for activity at the Ward Estate. "Yeah, boss. I'm sure. I've watched her like a hawk, and she's been hibernating in her mansion since her Christmas break began. You'd think she would have a date, attend a party, or something. But ... no."

"She went on an extensive shopping trip and met friends for lunch, but you missed it because you were locked up. I didn't like bailing you out, so don't let that happen again. No more tresspassing. Understand?"

"I understand, sir." Marco listened as his boss threatened to give the assignment to someone else.

"That's not necessary. I've got it covered. When she makes a move, I'll catch it on film. She has to leave the grounds sometime." He signed off, ended the call, and picked up his leftover turkey and dressing. "Okay, Rich Girl. You've got to give me a front-page story. I'll be back to my stakeout tomorrow even though it's freezing out there."

Chapter Eight

Tanner tapped his knuckles on Ward's home office door and stuck his head in. "You wanted to talk to me, sir?"

Alexander worked on his laptop dressed in a sweater and slacks, proving he was taking a leisure day. He pushed a couple of tabs, then closed his PC. "Yes, I do. Have a seat."

Tanner stepped into the room, surveying the décor. Impressive hardbacks filled the bookcases, trophies from hunting trips around the globe hung in strategic places, and several photos of famous people hung on the walls. The wooden furnishings added a masculine feel to the space. He eased into one of the chairs in front of Ward's desk. "Great office, sir. I didn't look around when I was here before."

"Joy loved displaying special moments in our lives by including photos and mementos in her décor." He leaned forward in his leather desk chair. "Tanner, thanks to your help, we may have located the firm that assigned Marco Thorne, the photographer, to follow Angelica. The company approved his work but not his stalker methods. He may face criminal charges for the drone incident. It could have been a case of manslaughter if you hadn't saved Angelica. I'm forever in your debt."

"I'm glad I was there." He crossed his ankles and relaxed. "It was a close call." He paused. "Is Thorne out on bail, or are they keeping him locked up?"

"I'm assuming he's posted bail by now. I haven't heard."

"Is that why you wanted to see me?"

"No. I've been watching you, Tanner. I admire your integrity and work ethic. I know you're completing your studies this spring, and I want to offer you a position with Ward Enterprises. I'd like you to consider taking the lead position at the tanzanite mine in Kenya." Ward leaned back in his tufted desk chair.

"Wow. I'm surprised you'd consider me for the position and truly honored." Tanner took a deep breath and blew it out.

"If you choose to take the position, the job must be completed within two and a half to three years. It's going to flood, making mining impossible. You've seen the land and understand the challenges it presents. I'll see you're well compensated and given a percentage of the amount mined as a bonus. Think about it for a few weeks, then call me."

"I'll do that. Thank you for considering me for the job." Tanner started to stand.

Ward held up his hand to stop him. "There's one more thing."

"Sure, Mr. Ward." Tanner sat back down.

"I've given this a lot of thought, and I've come to a decision."

Tanner smiled nervously. "This sounds serious." He shifted in his chair.

"It is to me, personally. It's about Angelica." Ward reached into his desk and pulled out an envelope.

"You've been there for Angelica since the first day she came to live at the estate. You've watched out for her, doctored her scrapes, kept her out of trouble for years. From helping with science projects to being her dance partner, you unknowingly helped us raise her. You're her best friend and confidant, and I'm extremely thankful for you."

"She did keep things from being boring. That's for sure." Tanner smiled, remembering the times she got them both in trouble with her antics.

"Because of your oversight and watchful eye following Angelica all these years, I want to cover your educational loans as payment for all the hours you've spent with her." He held the envelope toward Tanner. "You've worked hard and deserve to be compensated for your time. I know Angelica can be a full-time job."

Tanner leaned forward in his chair. "Sir—"

Angie stepped into the office, slapped a piece of mail she'd signed for on her grandfather's desk, and faced Tanner. "Let me get this straight. I was a job to you! You were getting paid to be my friend? I guess you were the best choice since you already lived here. And to think I trusted you. I can't believe this!" She held up her hand when Tanner tried to speak.

With fire in her eyes, she turned to her grandfather. "Grand-Papa! You're paying him for watching over me because I'm such a handful? I heard you. But I can't believe you would stoop this low." She took a step back.

"Angelica!" Ward stood. His chair hit the wall behind him.

"I don't want to hear it. I guess your money can buy anything if it buys people." She looked at Tanner, slapped at the tears streaming down her cheeks, turned, and ran.

Tanner stood and started toward the door.

"Let her go. Give her a few minutes. She's too upset to be reasoned with." Ward pulled his desk chair forward, sat, and scrubbed his hands down his face.

Tanner turned and strode to the chair he'd vacated. "Sorry, sir." He ran his hand through his hair.

After a deep sigh, Ward looked at Tanner. "No, I'm sorry. This is my fault. She'll be okay. I'll explain it to her. You didn't know my intentions. Take a minute and text her. Tell her this was a surprise to you. I'll wait." Ward reached for the envelope Angie had delivered.

Tanner texted Angie and told her he'd see her before he left the estate. "I hope she doesn't turn her phone off. She was pretty upset."

"I know. She's hurt, and I'm the guilty party." Ward took a deep breath and blew it out. "Let's finish our meeting, shall we?"

"Yes, sir."

Ward picked up the envelope he'd prepared for Tanner. "Please take this and pay your loans. I appreciate everything you've done, and I'm proud of the man you've become. Consider it a graduation gift." He held it out to Tanner again.

"I appreciate your generosity, but I don't want payment for the time I've spent with Angie. She's my friend, and no amount of money is worth jeopardizing our relationship. Can we wait on this until we talk again?" Tanner held his gaze.

"I'll hold it for you until we discuss the job in Kenya. Let me clear things up with Angelica." Ward opened the desk drawer and put the envelope inside.

Tanner stood. "I appreciate the job offer. I'll pray about it and call you for an appointment."

"Thanks, Tanner."

He left Ward's office and checked his phone. No texts. He wasn't surprised. The job offer was an amazing opportunity—

a future with Ward Enterprises. *Alexander Ward believes in me.* But knowing Angie was hurting drained the excitement from the moment. He wanted to explain, to ease her pain as he'd done through the years. But this wasn't a scraped knee.

When he called her, it went straight to voicemail. "Angie, please call me and let me explain. You've always trusted me— don't stop now."

Angie's cell vibrated with another message, but she didn't answer it. She'd never felt so betrayed, so wounded. She was devastated. All her special memories included Tanner. He knew her hurts, her hopes, her dreams, but it was all an act. He was earning a paycheck.

And her grandfather had stepped over the proverbial line, had been over the line her whole life. What could she do about it now? Fear of being alone gripped her. Now, she'd never know if her friends were with her because they wanted to be or because they'd been hired.

Her tears wouldn't stop. Every time she replayed her grandfather's words, her heart broke a little more.

"Miss Angie, are you here?" Sarah knocked on her bedroom door before opening it slowly. "Oh, Miss Angie. What's wrong? Your makeup is a mess, and your eyes are swelling."

"I just had my heart broken." Angie tried to keep from sobbing in front of her assistant. "Could you get me something to drink? Some sweet tea, maybe."

"Sure, and I'll get you an ice pack for those eyes." She started out the door, then turned back. "I came to tell you your grandfather wants to see you right away. What shall I tell him?"

Angie didn't answer.

"I'll get that drink for you." Sarah hurried out.

Blowing her nose and wiping her face only made room for more tears. She had to think—to plan. Stalling for time, Angie slipped into her pajamas and climbed into bed with her makeup remover, a box of tissues, and the remote control.

Sarah slipped in on quiet feet. "You may be comfortable, but your face still appears distraught. May I add some popcorn to this tray, Miss Angie?"

"Distraught. I haven't heard that word used in a long time. Popcorn sounds good. And please tell my grandfather I'm in bed. Tell him I'm distraught and deeply wounded. It'll sound good coming from you. Ask him if we could meet in a couple of months."

"Months?"

"Yes, months. He'll get the message." She teared up again.

"Okay. Don't cry. I'm sure this will pass."

The doorbell rang.

Sarah looked at Angie but didn't move.

"Answer it. But I'm not seeing anyone. Tell them I'm in bed. No—use one of your words, like 'indisposed.'"

"Yes, Miss Angie."

Angie blew her nose and wiped the mascara off with makeup remover.

After a few moments, Sarah stuck her head in the door again. "Miss Angie. Are you certain you won't be swayed? Tanner's at the door."

Her tears started again. "I won't be swayed." She shook her head.

Sarah went back to the door before returning once more. "He asked that you listen to his messages on your phone." She waited. "Shall I have Maria prepare a salad for you, Miss Angie? Maybe a chef salad or a Caesar?"

"Chef salad would be great. Thanks."

"You're welcome. I'm sorry you're sad. Do pray about your worries. Letting the Lord carry the other end lightens the load." Sarah retrieved her used tissues and tossed them into the trash before slipping out of her room.

Her phone buzzed again. Tanner. Hearing his Hummer leave the estate brought another flood of tears. She was truly alone. Everything sure and solid in her life had been jerked from under her feet. Her heroes had fallen. She couldn't see her way forward.

"Had you accepted the check?" Dylan plopped onto his bed and took a swig from his water bottle.

"No. He was handing it to me when she came in. But she exploded on both of us—not giving either of us a chance to say a word. I've never seen her so angry." Tanner paced the room.

"Okay, let me recap. You two had a great time at the party, ending with a kiss under the kissing ball. Then you exchanged gifts, and things were great until Mr. Ward decided to pay you for being there for Angie all these years. Right?"

"Yeah, that about sums it up. We talked about the paparazzi problem. Then he offered me a job in Kenya for the next three years running a tanzanite mine, which is an amazing opportunity. I thought the meeting was over, but he had one more item on his agenda. That's when things went south. He wanted to cover all my school loans as payment for being Angie's friend all these years. You should have seen Angie's face when she heard him. She was livid."

Tanner checked his phone. "I've sent several messages, but her phone's off. I stopped by before I left the estate, but she wouldn't see me. Her assistant said she was in bed crying." Tanner sat on his bed and covered his face with his hands.

"You have to give her some time. I'd continue reaching out to her until she opens communication again. Her world has been turned upside down, breaking her heart in the process. Gramps blew it big time. And she thinks you've deceived her. But she's strong, and strong people walk away if they feel unwanted, undermined, or deceived, as in this case. They won't try to fix it, and they definitely won't beg." Dylan took another drink of water. "Time and space are the only things that will help right now."

"How did you get so smart?"

"Psychology 101." Dylan smiled. "Don't worry too much. Her grandfather will tell her you knew nothing about the check. It'll take the sting out of the situation as far as you're concerned. If I were you, I'd pray about it. You have deep feelings for her, my friend."

"How can you be so sure, oh mighty counselor?"

"One sure sign is that when she's hurting, you're in pain too."

"You're probably right. But I can't let it go anywhere. She's the princess, and I'm the pauper."

"But this isn't medieval times. You're both millennials—a new breed of free thinkers. Risk takers. Give love a chance, my friend." Dylan tossed his empty water bottle into the trash can as if it were a basketball net. "I hit it again!" He pumped his fist into the air.

"Doesn't take much to make you happy." Tanner rubbed the back of his neck, then rotated it to get the kinks out. He checked his cell for a message. Finding none, he texted Angie again.

Angie spent the morning taking down the Christmas tree in her suite. She boxed the centerpiece from the middle of her table and pulled the Christmas dishes out of the kitchen cabinets.

She picked up the house phone and dialed the kitchen. "Maria, would you ask Jane to bring the boxes for the Christmas dinnerware to my suite and pack them for me? I have my decorations and tree ready to be stored if the staff can take care of those too."

"Absolutely."

Angie thanked her. She was stalling until her grandfather left for the office, knowing he wouldn't go out too early because of the icy streets. He usually waited until the roads had been traveled and salt had been administered before calling his driver.

When Angie saw the limo leave with her grandfather, she exited her suite. Entering the large living room with its ornate windows, Persian rugs, and expensive paintings incited a longing for the days when laughter filled the space. She ached for her grandmother as she stored the expensive ornaments she had cherished, thinking of the way she'd always dressed as if guests could drop in at any time. Wearing a small strand of pearls, pump heels, and a thin sweater draped across her shoulders, she could have entertained royalty at a moment's notice.

The staff worked quietly as they removed the Christmas decorations and dismantled the tree in the living room. The absence of Christmas music added to the solemnness of their task.

"Miss Angie, there's a present under here." Ellis picked up the small package covered in ornate wrapping and a sparkling bow and placed it in her hands.

It was the gift Mason Malone had left for her, which she'd

forgotten all about. Opening it and finding a bottle of her favorite cologne, she sighed. The gift was expensive, but since she had plenty and didn't want to be reminded of Mason, she handed it back to Ellis.

"Give this to your sweet wife. I have plenty of cologne, and she'll love it."

"Thank you, Miss Angie. Her birthday is in two weeks."

"It will make a great birthday present. Don't mention it came from me. Be a hero."

With a grin, he tucked it under his arm and headed for the kitchen.

Angie had the ladder moved to the front door, locked the door, and climbed the rungs. Reaching for the kissing ball, she dislodged it from its perch as Maria entered the foyer.

"Maria, would you dispose of this for me?" Angie handed it to another employee, who took it to Maria.

"Sure. Are you taking all the decorations down today, Angie?"

"No. I want the estate to resemble a winter wonderland. I'll remove the red bows on the staircase and replace them with silver. These foyer trees will be redecorated with pale blue and silver. I'm bringing out the toy soldiers to replace the sleigh of presents, and we'll add more snowflakes too. It'll be beautiful."

"I have no doubt." Maria stepped closer to her. "Angie, you've worked all morning. Would you like some lunch?"

"That would be great. I want to put away my grandmother's delicate ornaments and her village scene. I'll have my lunch in the living room by the fireplace. The staff can complete the storing of the lights, trees, and garland." She climbed down the ladder. "Would you mind putting away the Bethlehem scene this afternoon?"

"I'd be glad to." She returned to the kitchen.

Angie gave Ellis four large wreaths decorated in silver and

light-blue ornaments and shiny ribbons for the gate and the front doors. "Please change the wreaths for me. We may need to put the other wreaths in the garage for a few days since it rained this morning. They'll need to dry before they're stored."

"I can do that. Are you staying in here, Miss Angie?"

"Yep, having lunch by the fireplace."

The employees brought the outside décor into the foyer to dry and store, letting in freezing air each time they opened the door. But a roaring fire battled the chill so that the living room stayed warm and toasty.

Maria brought Angie a tray. "Here's your lunch."

"I appreciate it. You did a wonderful job managing the estate through the Christmas season. I love your attention to detail."

"Thanks." Maria paused. "You need to talk, Angie?"

Angie's eyes threatened tears. "Tanner told you what happened?"

"Yes. He hates to see you cry. I'm here if you need a listening ear," Maria said.

"Thanks, but no."

"I've heard it said, 'Tears are words your heart can't say.'" She touched Angie's shoulder. "If you change your mind, I'll be in the kitchen."

Angie listened to a message Tanner had left on her phone even though she wasn't ready to answer his calls.

"I'm still waiting to hear from you. Please trust me, Ang. About the event for the vice president, I sent two suggested agendas for the evening to your grandfather's email. I'm sure he'll let us know which one he prefers. I'll be there Saturday afternoon to help with any last-minute details."

After waiting another hour so Tanner would be in class, she left a message on his phone. "Things are on target with the event. It'll be successful. About what happened—I haven't talked to my grandfather yet. I was thinking about the scripture in Psalms you've mentioned before about being kicked in the gut. I need the Lord to help me catch my breath."

She left it at that, not knowing what else to say and not wanting to explain in a voicemail.

Her current conundrum was not knowing what to say to Grand-Papa. She knew she couldn't avoid him much longer. He'd hurt her. Their relationship had shifted, and her next steps would be tenuous. In a perfect world, love and trust walked hand in hand, but this wasn't a perfect world.

"I mean it, boss. She hasn't left the mansion since Christmas. And I'm about frozen." Thorne shivered and pulled his coat collar tighter to shield himself from the wind.

"Surely she'll have plans for New Year's Eve. Stick it out. Get the scoop. It'll warm your bank account."

"If I don't freeze to death first. It's snowing again, and the limos are in the garage. I'm going to call it a night and start again tomorrow." He stood, brushing snow off his shoulders.

"Well, wear your long johns and suck it up—unless you want me to reassign her to Wilson. He's chomping at the bits to get his name in print." He laughed.

"That's not funny. I've paid a price for this story. I'll get her on the front page yet. She's mine. Goodbye, boss."

Thorne heard his boss laugh like a hyena as he ended the call.

Chapter Nine

In keeping with Ward tradition, Angie decided to join her grandfather for dinner on New Year's Day. She informed Maria of her decision so she'd set an extra plate. As per tradition, she dressed semi-formal. Arriving in the dining room before her grandfather, Angie took a seat, and when he stepped into the room, she rose.

"Angelica, I'm so glad you've joined me for dinner. I would have been lonely without you." He kissed her cheek and held her chair in his mannerly fashion.

"I didn't want you to start this new year alone, Grand-Papa. We Wards keep our traditions, and having dinner together on New Year's Day is one of them." She placed her linen napkin on her lap and took a sip of water. "I think they're ready to serve us. You want to say a prayer?"

Ward offered thanks for their food and asked for the Lord's blessings on the new year, and then soup and salads were served. For a few minutes, the only sound was the silverware hitting bone china.

Ward set his salad plate aside and leaned back in his chair. "Angelica, I owe you a profound apology."

"Grand-Papa, we don't have to talk about this now if you'd rather wait." She tasted her soup and reached for the salt. "It's New Year's Day."

"I don't want to go another minute without explaining myself to you. Please hear me out."

Angie put her soup spoon down and faced him.

"Though I had several items on my agenda for my meeting with Tanner, the last matter I addressed was the one you heard when you entered the office." He looked down before meeting her gaze again.

"First, I want to make it clear that my desire to compensate Tanner for watching over you was a surprise to him. He knew nothing about my plan. Second, I'm grateful for the way he has been there for you through the years. When he saved your life last summer, I wanted to bless him. His college loans have mounted, and I'd like to pay those expenses. He grew up here at the estate—albeit at the other end of the property. He's not family, but he holds a special place in my heart. You should know he refused the money. I'm still holding the check."

Jane entered the dining room and delivered their entrées under silver domes.

Ward raised his hand. "Leave the domes for now, Jane."

"Yes, sir." Jane returned to the kitchen.

"Grand-Papa, I have no problem with you wanting to fund his education. The issue was that it sounded like you'd hired him to be my friend—to watch out for me ever since I'd come to live at the estate. And it looked like he was accepting the check. I felt deceived. It caused me to question if his friendship was all an act performed for a paycheck. I felt you had bought a playmate for me."

Ward grabbed her hand. "Please forgive me, Angelica. That wasn't my intention. I would never purposefully cause you heartache or pain."

Angie's eyes filled with tears. "I've always feared being alone—maybe because I was orphaned. I don't know. But when I entered your office, I felt like the two people I truly trusted had betrayed me. I was devastated." She used her napkin to wipe her tears before continuing. "Then, the people I usually talk to weren't there, and I realized I was alone in this world. Private schools and stalking paparazzi have reinforced the protective bubble you put around me. I understand the reasons. These kinds of things come with wealth and success. But it's lonely at the top of the totem pole."

"Please forgive me, Angelica. I wasn't aware you felt like this, and with the check incident, I've hurt you, and I am sorry." He waited.

Angie sighed. "It'll take me some time to process, but I forgive you, Grand-Papa." She squeezed his hand. "Why didn't Tanner accept the check?"

"He said he didn't want compensation for his time with you, and he wouldn't jeopardize your friendship. The check is still in my desk drawer."

Friendship.

She took a moment to let that soak in. "It's kind of you to want to pay his loans, Grand-Papa. He should accept your offer."

Ward leaned back in his chair. "I think you need to tell him to accept the gift."

"Consider it done." She reached over and removed the dome covering his entrée. "Let's eat."

"Steak. It does look good." He picked up his fork. "Are you okay now?"

"I will be. This experience has caused me to do some serious soul-searching. It's zapped my strength." She hesitated. "It'll take me a little time, but I'll be okay."

"That's fair." He picked up his iced tea. "I love you, my dear."

"I know, and I love you too, Grand-Papa."

They enjoyed their dessert and Kenyan coffee in a relaxed atmosphere.

Ward hugged her before he left the dining room. "Happy New Year, Angelica."

"Thank you." She kept her seat and finished her coffee as she watched the fire crackling in the fireplace. *I hope it's a happy new year.*

Angie took a deep breath and let it out before calling Tanner. "Hi."

"Well, hello. Happy New Year, Angie."

"I hope you have a happy New Year, Tanner. I had dinner with Grand-Papa." She tucked her hair behind her ear.

"I'm glad. Did he explain what happened?"

"Yeah."

"How did it go? Are you okay?"

"It was hard to hear, but I'll be fine. This week has been tough."

"I know it has. Anything I can do?"

"Accept the check—pay your school loans."

"No."

Angie ended the call and smirked about hanging up on Tanner. She relaxed by the fire and drank one of the black-currant sodas Tanner had given her. Thinking in depth about her next moves, she decided to apply herself, finish this year, then move to an apartment—or maybe a condo for the fall semester—and make some friends. She needed to broaden her circle of relationships as part of her plan to pick herself up by her bootstraps.

～

Tanner ran his fingers through his hair as he dialed Angie's number. On the fourth ring, she answered.

"Hi, Tanner."

"Hello. Thanks for taking my call. Your grandfather approved the first agenda I sent him for the vice president's party. How's it going with the music?"

"Great. The group is very talented. I met with them and hired the ensemble on the spot. They're excited to sing and play for the vice president, and I'll compensate them for their time and talent. They've requested a photo with the VP. I'm sure we can swing it."

"Sounds great. He'll love it. Have you told your grandfather?"

"Not yet. But I will. Their gifts have arrived, and everything else is arranged. It'll be a successful evening."

"Good work, Ang."

"Did you get the check and pay your loans off?"

"Not yet."

Silence.

"Angie? I know you're smiling. It's not funny ..." The line went dead.

"She can be exasperating sometimes." Tanner opened his laptop.

"At least she's talking to you again," Dylan said. "I'm glad my fiancé isn't temperamental like her."

"Angie isn't temperamental. Maybe a little high-maintenance, but she has reason to be withdrawn after what happened." He searched for the document he'd been working on. "You ready for your wedding? You only have a couple days."

"Five days, to be exact. I'm ready, but I think Amy's getting nervous."

"That's normal, right?" Tanner reached for a water bottle on the table. "She just has a lot of details to take care of in the last few days before the wedding. She'll be fine."

"I hope you're right."

"Well, I'm the best man. And I know these things." Tanner tried to sound convincing.

"And how many times have you been a best man?"

Tanner grinned. "It's my first time."

Angie tapped on her grandfather's office door and entered slowly. She'd learned her lesson about barging into his office unannounced and didn't want to repeat the performance.

"Your gifts for the vice president, his wife, and the engaged couple have arrived. Do you want to open them and see if they meet your approval before they're wrapped?"

"Yes, please. I want to make sure they're as quality as they appeared online."

Angie put them on a side table. "I have some special music lined up for the event. The musicians are from Kenya and will be singing in Swahili."

"That's a splendid idea. They'll enjoy hearing their native language. Good thinking." She turned to leave. "Tanner will be here to host with you, right?" he asked.

"Yes. He's the best man at his friend's wedding on Friday night, but he'll arrive by noon on Saturday before our foreign guests arrive."

"That's good. I appreciate the work you've done." He smiled.

"*Hakuna matata.* No problem." She saluted and left the office.

As Angie surveyed the decorations and the table settings, her phone rang.

"Ang, you're not going to believe this!"

"What?"

"She didn't walk down the aisle."

"What did she do? Run?"

"The other way! Dylan was jilted."

"A runaway bride! You're kidding ... right?"

"I wish I was. It was bad, really bad."

"What happened? Dylan's a catch, a handsome soon-to-be lawyer from a great family. What was she thinking?"

"That's just it. No one knows. Dylan is heartbroken, and their parents are humiliated. The church was packed. They'd spent a bundle."

"I feel bad for him."

"So do I."

"What did everybody do? Just go home?"

"Some did. Dylan's dad invited the crowd to the reception hall to have dinner, and most people stayed for the meal. I think they felt sorry for Dylan and for both families involved. I took Dylan out to eat and helped him cancel their honeymoon. We're still at the restaurant. He stepped away to speak to his dad."

"I'm glad you were there for him. That's so sad."

"He's struggling."

"Sorry."

She paused.

"Tanner, did you pay your loans off?"

"Goodbye, Ang."

Angie laughed out loud and hung up. He'd beaten her to the punch and said goodbye first ... this time.

When Tanner pulled to the gate, security officers were checking a delivery truck with flowers. He put his truck in park and watched the process, glad they were being thorough. Once cleared to enter the grounds, Tanner pulled his Hummer to his mom's end of the estate and spent a few moments with her.

People were coming and going, pushing carts of flower arrangements through the foyer when Tanner arrived at the ballroom door. He had déjà vu. Leaning against the doorframe, he watched Angie directing traffic like a crossing guard. She was in her element—chandeliers overhead, imported carpet under her feet, and a project in front of her.

Tanner waited. They hadn't talked in person since the office incident the day after Christmas.

"Well, Zarello. I'm glad you decided to show up." She looked at her watch. "You're an hour late."

"Hello, Angie. It's good to see you too."

"You like how the room is looking?" She turned toward the ballroom.

"It looks amazing. Has the food arrived?"

"Due anytime now." She checked the time on her cell.

"I guess it's early yet."

"I staggered the delivery times for security reasons so the trucks could be searched before our guests arrive. The food will be coming through the kitchen."

"Good plan. It looks like you've got it covered. I'm going to grab a Coke. You want one?"

"That would be great, thanks."

"Edward, I was getting concerned. You're a bit late." Angie faced her caterer.

"My apologies, Miss Ward. An employee stood me up. I had to find a replacement at the last minute. We'll get this set up in time. Do you want the food arranged like your grandmother used to prefer?"

"No, I've adjusted a few things. I have a diagram to show you. It makes life a little easier for me and my grandfather. You've served the Wards so well through the years. That's why I called you again."

"I won't let you down." Edward started barking orders to his staff, who rolled in carts of desserts and the makings of a coffee bar.

Angie followed him into the room. "We're setting up the desserts on the tables by the far wall. The drink station will be on the table to the left. Some of my people will assist so we can stay on schedule."

Tanner pushed a cart of soft drinks into the room. Jane carried two bakery boxes. Maria followed with a display of serving utensils.

"Thanks for hiring my company again, and I appreciate the help getting set up." The caterer gave instructions to his staff and turned to his newest hire. "Hey Mark, don't just stand there staring at Miss Ward. We have work to do, and we're running out of time."

Tanner heard the caterer and spun around to check out the employee. A ball cap hid part of his face, but the small device attached to the lanyard above his name tag revealed his ultimate goal.

Mark. "Marco Thorne!" Tanner yelled and rushed to capture the paparazzi.

Thorne saw him coming and spun into action. He pushed a cart of coffee pots and cups toward Tanner. He turned, his eyes wide as he assessed the banquet room. Stealing a knife off the tray in Maria's hand, he slung it at Tanner. As Tanner dodged the blade, Thorne caught Angie in a headlock. She screamed as she struggled to get free. Staff members scrambled away from the perpetrator and then froze, watching the standoff. When Tanner moved toward Angie, Thorne tightened his hold on her throat.

Tanner skidded to a halt. "No! Don't hurt her!"

"I won't hurt her. Don't you understand? She needs me! I'll make her famous, and her story will make my career. So back off, Jack!" He scanned the room.

Angie's eyes were wide with panic as she struggled against his grip. Staring at Tanner, a tear ran down her cheek. When he started moving toward the door, she sucked in a breath.

"You're not thinking, Thorne," Tanner said. "This will get you a story, all right. But it'll be about you committing a crime and facing a judge. You don't want to do this. It will end your career." Tanner tried to keep him distracted as he eased closer to Angie.

"Don't come any closer," Thorne demanded.

Tanner stopped, slowly reached into his back pocket, and pulled out his pocket knife. He opened it with a flick of his wrist behind his back. "Let her go, man. You're scaring her."

Sirens sounded in the distance.

"You called the police?" Thorne looked back as they neared the door. Tanner threw his knife, hitting him in the thigh.

Thorne yelled and grabbed his leg, giving Tanner the break he needed. He lunged for Angie, jerking her out of Thorne's grasp. Pulling the knife from his leg, the perpetrator slashed Tanner's arm. Ellis knocked the knife from his hand and apprehended him, preventing an escape. Blood ran down Thorne's leg as he was escorted out of the ballroom. Dallas police charged into the foyer, cuffed Marco Thorne, and recited his rights.

Angie was on the floor crying.

"Are you hurt, Ang?" Tanner started checking for injuries. He saw blood on her clothes and inspected her for cuts.

"I'm not hurt." She wiped her eyes. "That is, unless you're talking about the weight of your body squashing mine." Looking down, she saw the source of the blood. "Tanner, you're bleeding." She grabbed his arm.

"He cut me with my own knife when I rescued you." He stood and helped her to her feet. "I don't think it's a deep cut." He rolled his shirt sleeve up to see the wound.

"Maria, Tanner's bleeding." Angie looked at the cut. "Tanner, go to the kitchen and get the wound cleaned up so we can see if you need stitches."

Maria hurried to assist.

"You sure you're okay, Ang?" Tanner took her hand.

"I'm still in shock, but I'll be fine. Get your cut taken care of." She squeezed Tanner's hand before he left the room.

Using her shoulder, Angie wiped the tears still dampening her face. Sarah brought a cloth to clean the blood off Angie's hands. Once seated, a police officer took pictures of her neck, the knife, and the blood on the floor.

Angie took a deep breath and surveyed the room. The episode had halted all progress. "Edward, have your people get things set up. Tell them to enter through the other hall. Our staff will clean up this blood after the police release the scene. Hopefully, it'll be before our guests arrive."

Her staff helped the caterer while she answered the investigator's questions. The word 'stalker' heightened her anxiety as the officer told her what they found in the photographer's apartment. "He had photos of you all over the walls of one room. This guy was obsessed with you, Miss Ward. He may need a mental evaluation."

Cold chills rose on her arms. She'd seen things like this on cop shows, but this time she was the one whose life was in danger. When the police finished questioning her, she checked on Tanner's injury. With no stitches required, he was bandaged and questioned by the police officers.

Seeing blood on her clothes, Angie hurried to her suite to change. When the door clicked behind her, she backed up against the door, slid down to the carpet, and sobbed. Thorne's grip on her body and the fear etched on Tanner's face were branded in her mind. The nightmare had happened so quickly. The gravity of the attack and potential outcome played over and over in her mind like a movie clip.

When her tears subsided, she washed her face, changed clothes, and hurried back to the ballroom. Members of the Ward family didn't allow attacks to scare them. They sucked it up, held their heads high, and pressed forward. With swollen eyes, an absence of makeup, and trembling hands, she stepped back into the scene of the crime and went to work. She was a Ward, and the Ward constitution flowed through her veins.

"Are you okay, Angelica? I was horrified to learn Thorne had invaded our private residence again." Alexander Ward put his arm around her shoulders. "Charges are being filed and he has jail time in his future. It won't happen again."

"That's good to hear. I have to admit, it shook me pretty good." She paused, fighting tears. "Honestly, the fear on Tanner's face told me I was in serious danger. But I'm focusing on this event now, and I'll think about the incident later. Tanner will be back soon. Once he arrives, we'll get this party started."

Ward kissed her cheek. "I have total confidence in your planning. With you and Tanner hosting, it will be a splendid occasion."

The officers released the scene, leaving them with less than an hour to clean before their guests arrived. Angie stared at the blood on the floor and froze.

With one look at Angie's face, Tanner spun into action. Barking orders to the staff, he had everyone moving like a film on fast-forward. He stepped close to Angie, took her hand, and led her out of the ballroom.

"Sarah, would you get Angie a cold Coke? She needs a dose of caffeine."

Sarah hurried to the kitchen to comply.

"Let's sit on the couch for a few minutes, Angie." He sat next to her, rubbed her hand, and spoke softly. "Drink some cold soda and relax for a minute."

"Okay." She accepted the drink from Sarah.

"Take a deep breath and blow it out."

She followed his instructions. "I could have died today, Tanner."

"I know, but you're safe now. The threat has passed. He's behind bars and won't see the light of day for a long time if Alexander Ward has his way."

She attempted to smile. "He can be a bulldog when the occasion presents itself." She drank more of her Coke. "I'm feeling better now. Thanks."

"Listen, we've got this. Go to your suite, take a shower, put your knock-my-socks-off evening gown on, and meet me in the foyer in forty-five minutes."

After placing her drink in his hand, she stood. "You can finish my Coke."

He stood and watched her walk away. He'd never seen her so shaken.

When the limousines arrived, the fanfare began. Alexander Ward stood at the front doors of the estate flanked by Angie and Tanner, both dressed in formal attire—he in a tux and Angie in a tanzanite-blue floor-length gown with a scooped neckline that showed off her Africa necklace and tanzanite bracelet she'd received for Christmas.

Two employees rolled out the red carpet for the first limo carrying the vice president and his wife. Kenya's national anthem played from the outside speakers as Ward escorted their friends through the front doors.

Tanner and Angie joined in the traditional greetings of the vice president and the dignitaries in his entourage while other guests were vetted at the gate for security reasons. Within twenty minutes, the ballroom was bustling with Kenyans enjoying themselves.

Tanner stepped to the microphone to introduce Alexander Ward, who welcomed their special guests. Soft music played as dinner was served. The vice president seemed to love the silver domes and the flair of the presentation.

"Alexander, I must have some of these for dinners at my residence."

Ward smiled. "That can be arranged."

The food was delicious, the setting was amazing, the linens and candles provided a formal touch, and the silver and crystal reflected the sparkle of the chandelier. The décor resembled a stroll through a winter wonderland. As their guests enjoyed their desserts with Kenyan chai, the Kenyan musicians performed three numbers.

Saitoti stood and applauded when the first words rang out. "I love hearing Kiswahili."

"It was Angelica's idea," Ward said. "She thought you and your wife would enjoy their musical numbers."

Absorbing their presentation, Saitoti smiled throughout. "A splendid performance." Saitoti applauded, stood, and greeted the young people in Swahili before posing for photos.

"You're a genius. He loved it, Ang," Tanner whispered in her ear.

"My grandfather looks pretty impressed. Can you carry the gifts to the platform when they finish taking pictures?"

"Sure."

She loaded his arms, being careful to protect the wrappings and his wounded arm. "I'll give them to Grand-Papa in the order he requested."

"Sounds like a plan."

When the musical guests left the stage, Angie and Tanner moved to Ward's side and assisted him with the presentation of gifts.

Vice President Saitoti stood. He spoke eloquently to his

guests, honoring his daughter and his soon-to-be son-in-law before giving a moment to allow their guests to greet those gathered. The speeches were kind but lengthy.

The vice president brought the evening to an end. "It is difficult to find proper words of appreciation for the evening we have shared. The food was *tamu sana*—very delicious. The Kenyan music was delightful, and the gifts splendid. My friend, Alexander Ward, you have blessed us. And we are grateful."

Ward stood and embraced the vice president, then greeted his wife.

"Tanner, let's offer chai again before the evening ends."

"I'm right behind you, Ang."

They worked in tandem, serving their guests until the last one departed.

"That was a wonderful evening. You did a superb job. Saitoti was impressed. Thank you both." Ward picked up a piece of pie as he slowly headed toward his upstairs suite. "Good night to you both." He took a few steps, then paused. "And your checks are in the mail."

"Checks? We didn't know we were getting paid. Thank you, and see you tomorrow, Grand-Papa." She watched him go, then turned to Tanner. "Will you roll up the red carpet? It's supposed to rain tonight. I'll let the staff know the ballroom is ready to be cleared." Angie turned toward the kitchen.

"Sure. Are you coming back in here?"

Angie hesitated. "Yeah. I want a cup of that chai. Want to join me?"

"Okay. Get us two mugs while you're in the kitchen. This china is pretty delicate."

"I know what you mean." Angie prepared their Kenyan tea, adding sugar and stirring.

"I can't believe you guys don't have a push-button,

retractable red carpet installed." Tanner slapped his hands together, brushing dirt from them.

She turned and handed him his mug. "You think we have many royal guests?"

"Well, it could come out automatically when you arrive, Your Highness." He laughed.

"Now that would be overkill." She noticed the staff entering the room. "Let's move to the living room and let them work here." She sat at the end of the couch, and Tanner took the chair closest to her.

"How's your war wound? And when did you learn to throw a knife like that?"

He touched his arm. "It's fine. Throbbing a little. About the knife throwing, I was a boy scout in a past life."

She smiled. "Yeah, right."

"Are you still struggling from the attack this afternoon?"

"I've tried to put it out of my mind, but it replays like a bad movie. I was scared. Petrified. In the moment, I felt like I'd been in his grip for a long time. But it was only a matter of minutes—long minutes." She paused. "I'm just glad he's out of the picture—pun intended." She looked at the fire. "Thanks."

"Welcome."

"How's Dylan?" She took a sip of her chai.

"Changing the subject?" Tanner set his cup on the end table and sighed. "He's struggling. He hasn't heard a word from Amy, but her family has. She hasn't offered a reason for her actions nor an apology. It's hit him pretty hard."

"He's been kicked in the gut." Angie cradled her mug, enjoying the warmth.

"Yeah, but he hasn't come up for air yet."

"Isn't he preparing to take the bar?"

"Yeah, in six weeks. He planned to get married, pass the

bar, then set up a private practice or join his dad's firm." He reached for his chai and took a sip. "This stuff is good."

"Yeah, I like it."

"Are you okay, Ang? I've sensed a difference in you since Christmas, and today's incident has taken its toll." He held her eyes.

"This afternoon's incident will take some time to wear off." Pausing, she looked at the fire again and then caught his gaze once more. "I think I'd become too sure of myself. It's good for us pedestal dwellers to be reminded of how fragile life is. A good dose of reality never hurt anybody." She sipped her chai.

"Well, I'd like to turn the clock back and get a do-over." He ran his hand through his black hair. His brown eyes glowed with the reflection of the fire.

"We all want the impossible, Tanner." She put her mug on the coffee table and stood. "Thanks for your help tonight. It was a wonderful success."

"I didn't do much. You did all the heavy lifting. But we do make a pretty good team. Are you turning in now?"

"Yeah. My day started early."

"I'm here with my mom for the weekend. Have lunch with me tomorrow. I have something I want to talk to you about." He picked up her cup and stepped toward the kitchen.

She stared at him for a long moment, contemplating her answer. "Okay. Text me the time."

"If I can get a definite answer ..." He smiled.

"Good luck with that. Good night." She moved toward her end of the estate.

"Good night, Angie."

She raised her hand in a wave and kept walking.

Chapter Ten

The pristine kitchen smelled like chocolate. "Are those brownies?" Tanner smiled at his mom as Maria took the mugs from Tanner.

"How is she?" Maria asked.

"Guarded. Distant. She keeps changing the subject on me. She's put up some walls." He sat on a barstool and helped himself to a brownie his mom had just taken out of the oven. "I'm not sure about my next steps."

Maria set a glass of cold milk in front of him. "Pain has caused her to question who she can trust. She's protecting her heart, Tanner. You'll have to gain her confidence again."

"I'm trying, but I didn't do anything wrong." He stuffed the last of his brownie into his mouth.

"Once you've been alone like she has, the solitary feelings will hit hard. Give her time." She covered the plate of brownies. "She'll come around."

"Is this coming from experience, Mom?" He finished his milk.

"I've had my share of dark days. That's how I know she'll be okay."

"I hope you're right. I asked her to have lunch with me tomorrow. Can you make those chicken sandwiches she's so crazy about?"

"Yeah, I can. But why would you eat a sandwich you don't like?"

"With everything that's happened, I want to tell her about the job offer in Kenya. I don't want her to hear about it and think I was keeping it a secret."

"That's a good idea." She stopped working on the cellophane and stared at Tanner. "You're overly concerned. I guess the events of last week would make you cautious. But want to know what I think?"

Tanner met her gaze. "Yeah, give it to me straight."

"I think you need to tell yourself the truth." She wiped some crumbs he'd dropped.

"What do you mean? I haven't lied, Mom."

She moved closer and put her hand on his shoulder. "In the last couple of years, you've changed. I see the way you look at her. I noticed the fear on your face after you pulled her out of the lake. You light up when she enters the room. With all those pretty young ladies at the university you could date, you've not considered one of them. You're at Angie's beck and call—jumping through hoops to please her. You're in love with her, Tanner."

Tanner stood and had to grab the stool to keep it from hitting the floor. "Mom!"

"Drop the protective barrier for a minute and listen to your heart." She paused. "Let me ask you this. How would you feel if she started dating someone else? Think about it. She's embedded deep in your heart. You'd be devastated if you lost her to another man, and trust me, she is getting noticed."

Tanner righted the barstool, sat again, and scraped his hands down his face. He took a deep breath, blew it out, and hung his head. "I've tried not to love her. But she wove her way into my heart a long time ago." He faced his mom. "But it would never work. She's young with the world at her fingertips, and I'm way below her class, Mom. I'm not good enough."

"That's absurd. She's a mature young woman who loves you as her dearest friend. None of the things you're worried about matter to Angie. If you want more than friendship, you better make your move." She removed his dishes. "And fast."

"Yes, ma'am."

Light snow began to fall as Angie stared at the moon's glow on the lake. So much had happened since her fall into those waters. She'd given her heart to Tanner, planned to rush her education, become passionate about helping orphans, and survived a major clash with her grandfather. When she mixed in the threats from Marco Thorne, it was no wonder she was having trouble sleeping. She rubbed her arms to ward off the chill in her living room. Moving to her kitchen, she decided to make some hot chocolate to relax her nerves. But the Keurig took its time.

Questions stirred through her mind. *Will Marco Thorne be released again? Will another paparazzi take his place? What does Tanner want to talk to me about? Can I let my guard down to trust him again? Grand-Papa's limp is getting worse. Is something else wrong with him?*

The Keurig hissed, signaling her chocolate was ready. She took a sleep aid, sipped her chocolate, and asked the Lord to give her peace and direction as she drifted to sleep on her comfy couch.

"Morning, Sarah." Tanner greeted her as she entered the kitchen. "How's Angie this morning?" Tanner was eating breakfast with his mom in the kitchen.

"I went in earlier, but she's asleep on the couch. The sleep aid the doctor gave her was open on the kitchen cabinet. She's been having trouble sleeping since Christmas. What did you and Mr. Ward do to her? She's changed. She has only driven her new car twice. What happened?"

"We made her feel alone. Betrayed. But she misread the situation. And it left deep wounds." He stood and refilled his coffee.

"I'd say it did. Well, fix it, Tanner. Do something drastic if you have to." Sarah was adamant. "We want her smile back."

"I do too." *More than you know.*

The warm shower soothed Angie's body. She stood there, letting it wash over her, wishing it could smooth out the bumps in the road she was navigating. She wasn't ready to trust yet. Risking her heart took courage she didn't have.

With her hair washed and conditioned, she stepped out of the shower and slipped her fluffy robe on.

"Miss Angie, I put a breakfast tray on the vanity in your room for you to enjoy while you do your makeup and dry your hair."

"Thanks, Sarah."

"Tanner asked about you when I went for your breakfast tray."

Angie stuck her head out her bedroom door. "What did you tell him?"

"I told him you'd slept in this morning, and I fussed at him for hurting you."

"You didn't." Angie's eyes widened.

"Yes, I did." Sarah put her hands on her hips.

Angie laughed. "I'd like to have seen that." She took her time getting dressed since she had a couple of hours to kill before lunch. She chose some skinny jeans and a deep-blue sweater. Tanner had said it matched her eyes. With her journal in hand, she curled up in front of the fireplace in the regal living room of the estate to write her thoughts. Documenting her feelings helped her process the events she'd walked through—to find peace. The crackling of the fire was her background music. The warmth of the blaze encased her as she poured her heart out onto the pages and relaxed.

"What are you writing?" Tanner took a seat beside her. He wore his favorite jeans and a new sweater he probably got for Christmas.

"Oh, just some stuff. What's up?" She closed her journal, set it aside, and met his gaze.

"No, I'm curious. What have you written in that journal of yours?" He waited as she reopened the book.

Maria poked her head out the kitchen door. "Tanner, Angie, your lunch will be ready in twenty minutes."

"Thanks, Mom." He leaned forward and put his elbows on his knees. "I'm waiting. Read to me, Ang."

She turned to a page at the beginning of the journal. "Okay, if you're sure. Here it goes. On December twenty-sixth, I wrote *... Everything I've believed and thought true was based on a lie.*" She looked up at him, then continued. "Then I copied something I found on Pinterest. *It's not the future that you're afraid of. It's repeating the past that makes you anxious.* Another Pinterest saying said *... Pain changes you. It makes you build walls to protect yourself, trust less, overthink conversations more, and shut* *people out.*" She closed her journal and looked at the flames in the fireplace. "I've had those feelings. Thought those thoughts." She paused. "And I'm embarrassed by my reaction and inability to put it behind me." She looked at him. "Does that make sense?"

"It does." Tanner shifted his body toward her on the sofa.

She flipped to her last entry. "This is what I wrote today. *When you get hurt, finding your way back is tough. Deciding to get past the experience takes bravery because you could face that pain again. But staying in your misery isn't an option. So I've made a decision. I'm going to get up, reapply my lipstick, and try again.*" She closed the book and set it aside. "I also added a couple of scriptures I've been standing on as promises."

She looked up and sighed. "It's been tough, but I'm getting my footing again."

"It sounds like you've done a lot of thinking."

"I have. I should have heard what you and Grand-Papa had to say. Since I didn't, I went through a dark time. Being an orphan added to the darkness. I know I'm blessed. But without someone to share life with, I'm lonely. The Lord's my only constant. He's always there. This experience has reinforced that truth, and a sense of peace is slowly replacing my distress." She paused. "Sorry. That's probably more information than you bargained for."

Tanner leaned against the back of the couch. "Angie, I knew you were struggling. I've been concerned. You're one of the strongest people I know, but childhood traumas affect how you process pain."

"And you know this how?"

"Personal experience. When my dad abandoned us, he was angry because he had to watch me when he wanted to go to a bar with his friends. I'm sure there was more to the story I didn't understand, but the details of those moments are branded in my memory. He gave me a bowl of cereal for breakfast, made me a peanut butter sandwich for lunch, and told me it was on the cabinet. Then he left and never looked back—never returned. I was almost six, left home alone while I watched out the window all day for him to return."

He took a deep breath and let it out slowly. "When Mom came home after her shift, I was trembling, sobbing, and afraid. It was the longest day of my life. The feeling of abandonment haunted me with nightmares for years. I'll never forget it."

Angie put her hand on top of Tanner's. "I'm sorry. I knew Maria was a single mom, but I didn't know what you experienced. Why haven't you shared this with me before?"

"Because I didn't want your pity. I want you to know I understand some of what you've been feeling. No, I didn't lose both parents and didn't spend a year and a half undergoing surgery after surgery. But tragedies in our history affect us when painful situations occur. The paparazzi episode didn't help. It's added to your stress."

"You're right. I've cocooned myself at the estate while trying to regain my emotional strength. But I'm gun-shy. Wondering what's going to happen next."

"You're guarding your heart like you should, Ang. I understand, but don't close yourself off from the ones who care about you. I need to say something else." He paused and reached for her hand. "I've kept walls around my heart for years to keep from falling in love with you. I've clung to our friendship with a tight grip. I know our social standings don't mesh, but when you kissed me under the kissing ball, something changed. My feelings for you have escalated. I don't know where to go from here, but please don't shut me out."

He held his hand up to keep her from interrupting. "When we hurt you, your grandfather was so upset. I wanted to explain, to stop your tears, but you weren't receiving visitors. Not even me, your best friend. The staff was worried about you and upset with me and your grandfather. I'm so sorry we caused you pain. Please forgive us."

"Wait, you said something changed. What do you mean?"

"Lunch is served," Maria announced as she set their plated meal on the dining table.

Tanner stood and took her hand to help her up. They walked to the table, and he held her chair before sitting.

"Are you going to answer my question?" She laid her napkin across her lap.

"What about the tanzanite-blue Lexus I saw in the driveway?" He smiled.

"Well, I thought you might want to drive it after lunch."

"You thought right, Angelica. It's beautiful. Perfect for you."

"Thanks. I love it. It drives like a dream." Angie took a drink of her iced tea and fingered the condensation on the glass. "So what did you mean the staff was worried?" She furrowed her brow.

"They adore you and have been upset with me and your grandfather. They've threatened desperate measures if we don't repair the problems we caused."

Angie smiled. "Putting pressure on you, huh? Are they forcing you to sit here and eat with me? You don't like chicken salad." She took another sip of sweet tea, then set her glass by her plate.

Tanner grabbed her hand. "I'm not a fan of chick food. I'm here because I want things to be like they were at Christmas, Ang." He circled his thumb on the back of her hand. "The season was great. I loved seeing you so happy. You stepped into your role as the 'Lady of the Estate' with class and confidence."

"Thank you for saying that. I knew it would be a difficult holiday without Nana Joy. We missed her but made new memories."

"Your thoughtfulness and creativity helped your grandfather deal with her absence. Let me pray over our food." Tanner did so, including a plea for wisdom for forward steps in their relationship. He took a bite of his sandwich. "Who puts grapes in a sandwich?"

Angie laughed. "You're right. It's definitely chick food."

Eating in silence for a few minutes, Angie tried to relax and enjoy their time together. "Do your classes start this week?"

"Yeah. In two days, I start my final semester. I need to think about the future and what I'm going to do next. That's one reason I wanted to talk to you. In my meeting with your grandfather, he offered me the lead position on the mining project in Kenya."

Holding her sandwich midair, she froze. "But it would mean you'd move to Kenya." She spoke in a whisper.

"Yes, that's one drawback, but it would give me a chance to prove myself capable of seeing a project through from its inception to completion. It could make way for future assignments with Ward Enterprises. You've seen the site and heard about the project. What do you think?"

She took a drink of her iced tea before she spoke. "Offering you the position speaks highly of his confidence in you and your leadership skills. I have no doubt you'd do a stellar job." She paused, looking away.

"But—"

"But you would be so far away." She put her hand on his arm.

"It's called a long-distance relationship, Ang."

"Ten thousand miles is a really long distance."

"I know. But we can do anything we set our minds to. You'll be busy completing your education, and I'll have my hands full with the project. Time will fly." He put his hand on hers. "Think about what it can mean for the future. I have to prove myself."

Angie took a deep breath and let it out slowly. "I know you do. I was just hoping you'd be a little closer to home." She squeezed his arm and drew her hand back. "Let's finish our lunch and talk about it another time."

"Deal." He stuffed some chips into his mouth. "Don't you go back to school tomorrow?"

"Yeah, and I begin my classes at Southwestern University on Friday."

"Wait, you're doing both at the same time?"

"That's the plan. I was able to skip out of several classes because of my grade-point average and life experience. I'll be taking some sophomore classes this summer. I'm on a fast track to finish in less than three years."

"Wow. I had no idea. When did you decide this?" He finished his sandwich.

"After my drone episode. Coming close to death was a wake-up call. It shook me and clarified specific goals I want for my future, so I put the plan into motion."

"I'm proud of you, Ang. I want to be there when you're completely finished."

Jane entered quietly, took their plates, and refilled their tea glasses. "Your cheesecake will be out in a few minutes." She left them alone.

"Tanner, I'm confused. You said your feelings have changed toward me—toward *us*—then you talked about leaving the country for an extended period of time. How do you see this working out?"

"First, I need to know if your feelings for me are—"

"Zarrello, I've loved you since I was eleven, and you were my dance partner. My feelings for you have grown in intensity. Now that you've confessed feelings for me, I may be way ahead of you." She smiled.

"Not a chance. I know you love competition, but this can't be measured."

"Want to make a bet on that?" She winked.

"No. I've lost most of the bets we've made. I'm not risking this one."

Maria served them one large slice of cheesecake covered in strawberries and a sweet glaze with two forks. "Enjoy. Let me know if you want another slice."

"Thanks, Maria. It looks amazing." Angie didn't hesitate to take a bite. "And it tastes great."

"You're welcome." Maria went back into the kitchen, shutting the door behind her.

Tanner hit Angie's fork with his as she took her second bite. "May I have a bite, Miss Ward?" He teased.

"Okay, but only because there's more in the kitchen."

He laughed. "I love being with you, Angie. I always have. You're as amazing as you are beautiful."

"Are you surprised we weathered the braces, bad haircut, and acne stages of my life?"

"Well, I wasn't so handsome with my broken front tooth and mullet."

Her smile grew. "You were a vision." She fanned her face as if she were swooning. Their laughter filled the room.

Tanner reached for her hand and kissed the back of it, their frivolity forgotten. "So, what do you think about a long-distance relationship, Ang?"

"Absolutely. Yes. I've waited so long to let you know how I feel."

"I'd rather you showed me." He grinned.

Jane stepped into the dining room and delivered a tray with a silver dome over it. After removing their dessert plate, she left the room.

"What's this? It's lunchtime, Tanner. A formal presentation in the middle of the day isn't appropriate."

Tanner stood and removed the dome as he bowed with practiced flair. He reached for a ribbon attached to a round mound of greenery, held it up, and smiled.

"The kissing ball! How—? Why—?" She stood, pushing her chair back.

Tanner stepped closer and held the kissing ball above them. "How, you ask? I had the staff keep it refrigerated and watered. Why? Let me answer all your questions." He touched her cheek and slid his free hand behind her neck under her silky hair. He pressed his lips to hers in a whisper of a kiss, then slid his arm around her back and pulled her close, kissing her soundly.

The staff applauded and cheered. Tanner and Angie turned their heads to smile at their audience.

Standing in Tanner's warm embrace, Angie looked into his dark-brown eyes. "I think they're happy."

"I know I am."

Angie watched the staff return to the kitchen. She looked up to see the mistletoe dangling from Tanner's hand. "You can put the kissing ball down now."

"But what if I don't want to?"

"It has served its purpose. You have my heart, Tanner. You don't need the mistletoe anymore."

"I don't?"

She slid her hands around his neck, leaned close, shut her eyes, and answered with a heart-stopping kiss. When she felt both his arms embrace her, she knew the kissing ball had worked its magic … once again.

THE END

Acknowledgments

I'm so excited to share a new series with you. *The Kissing Ball* is a prequel to the Paradise Inn Series set in Kenya, the land of my calling.

Susan May Warren of Novel Academy taught me how to write Christian fiction. She is amazing. Donna Yarborough, my writing partner, has encouraged me every step of the way. I appreciate Karen Tankersly and Denica McCall for editing this manuscript. And, Linda Fulkerson at Scrivenings Press designed the cover and brought this novella to publication. I am forever grateful to these ladies.

To my tribe: Shelayne, Sharee, Shontel, Sheri, Johnnie, Jana, Judi, Karen, & Carol—you ladies are the best. You cheer me on during the writing process. You share my posts, sell books for me with each new release, and champion my work. You're the best!

My Mom and my family have been so supportive during this writing journey. 'Thank you' seems inadequate to express my gratitude to them. My grandchildren think I'm famous. They make me smile. Thank each of you ... Madi, Jake, Finley, Charlotte, Judah, Blakely, & Lyda.

Most of all, I thank the Lord for walking every step with me. His call on my life humbles me. His love keeps me going. I'm eternally grateful to represent Him in speaking and through the written word. May You be glorified, Lord.

About the Author

Shirley Gould is an inspirational speaker, an African missionary, and the author of The Sahar of Zanzibar, Escape From Timbuktu, and Sunset Over Swaziland. She's the founder of Kenya's Kids Home for Street Children, an orphanage in Kenya. Putting her personal experiences into her prose, she weaves adventurous tales, taking her readers to the wilds of Africa.

She makes her home in Nashville, Tennessee, where she enjoys time with her seven grandchildren, Madi, Jake, Finley, Charlotte, Judah, Blakely, and Lyda. Follow her writing journey and watch for another release at shirleygould.org.

The Sahar of Zanzibar

The African Skies Series - Book One

In a scary case of mistaken identity, Olivia Stone is threatened by Aga Kahn, a powerful Indian ruler, because she could pass as the twin of the missionary's deceased wife. Kahn calls her the Sahar of Zanzibar who has returned from the grave to torment him and demands that she leave the island or face his wrath. She'd come to exotic Zanzibar in search of adventure, but she experiences much more.

A handsome widower, Missionary Eli Deckland, steps between Olivia and the angry Indian, rescuing her. There's an instant connection between Olivia and Eli that escalates when he comes to her rescue again and again. Amid the chaos, Eli tries to prove Kahn murdered his late wife. After several attempts on Olivia's life, she's kidnapped. Eli joins the police to find her before it's too late.

As every moment passes, Olivia's life is in more danger... Will she be saved in time? If she is rescued, would it work between her and Eli? With an ocean keeping them apart, will their feelings fade? The answer is in the African skies …

Get your copy here:

https://scrivenings.link/thesaharofzanzibar

~

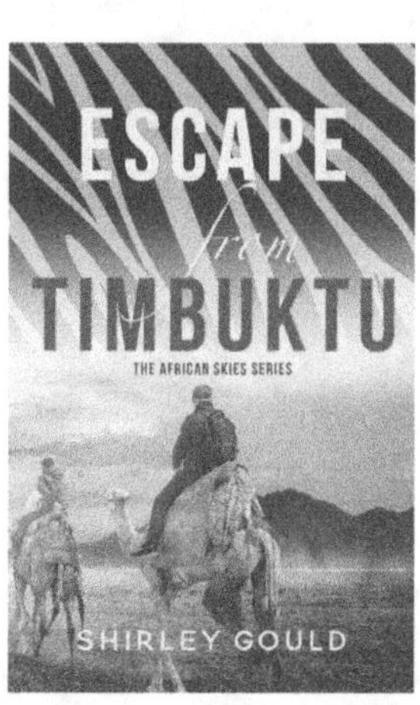

Escape from Timbuktu

The African Skies Series - Book Two

Elliana Bendale can't believe her first assignment as a photojournalist is in … well, Timbuktu.

Yes, it sounds remote, but it's an enchanting ancient city in West Africa, and if she does this right, this project could open the door to a world of exotic assignments. And even better—her translator is a ruggedly handsome Frenchman. What could be more exciting?

Beau de La Croix is not who he says he is. But posing as an interpreter enables him to gather intel about the terrorists threatening Timbuktu. No one needs to know he's a double agent—especially not Ellie.

Unfortunately, the number one enemy in the world has figured it out, and suddenly Ellie's photojournalist adventure includes dodging bullets, traveling down a crocodile-infested river, and literally running for her life.

What has Beau gotten her into? And if they survive, can she say goodbye to her hunky hero? Or is his life as a double agent too much excitement for a feisty Texas girl?

When Beau's worst fears come true, what will he do to save the feisty reporter he can't seem to shake?

Get your copy here:

https://scrivenings.link/escapefromtimbuktu

Sunset over Swaziland

The African Skies Series - Book Three

Grant writer Jocelyn Millender travels to Swaziland to get humanitarian aid for the devastated, disease-infested country. When war threatens, all travel is suspended. She's trapped, scared, and in danger.

Hearing about her life-threatening situation, Austin Bendale, a decorated soldier turned security services specialist, purchases a plane ticket and comes to the rescue. But things aren't as they seem. Hidden agendas are inciting riots, humanitarian funds are dwindling, and orphans are disappearing.

When you put one determined woman and a never-say-die hero in this life-and-death situation—using her gifts and his brawn—can they ignore the sparks between them, escape the chaos, solve the mystery, apprehend the guilty, and get across the border in time?

Because the sun is setting over Swaziland …

Get your copy here:

https://scrivenings.link/sunsetoverswaziland

Stay up-to-date on your favorite books and authors with our free e-newsletters.

ScriveningsPress.com

www.ingramcontent.com/pod-product-compliance
Lightning Source LLC
Chambersburg PA
CBHW071535120726
47907CB00014B/2196